Hanging Tree

When he came to, Slater was surprised to be alive.

Spitting dirt, he rolled over and sat up, wincing at the white-hot agony exploding in his skull. He gingerly felt the back of his head. Dried blood matted his hair.

The late afternoon shadows of the cottonwoods reached for him across the hardpack. Then he realized something besides cottonwoods was casting shadows, and he looked up to see two bodies hanging from one of the trees. One was Swope. Next to him was the half-breed outlaw. Why had they bothered hanging a dead man? Slater had no idea. He'd given up trying to figure people out a long time ago.

They had made one mistake by leaving Slater alive, then made another by not confiscating his horse and weapons. . . .

Also by Dale Colter

The Regulator
Diablo at Daybreak
Deadly Justice

Published by
HARPERPAPERBACKS

DALE COLTER

THE REGULATOR

DEAD MAN'S RIDE

HarperPaperbacks
A Division of HarperCollins*Publishers*

HarperPaperbacks   *A Division of* HarperCollins*Publishers*
          10 East 53rd Street, New York, N.Y. 10022

Copyright © 1991 by HarperCollins*Publishers*
All rights reserved. No part of this book may be used or
reproduced in any manner whatsoever without written
permission of the publisher, except in the case of brief
quotations embodied in critical articles and reviews. For
information address HarperCollins*Publishers*,
10 East 53rd Street, New York, N.Y. 10022.

Cover art by Miro

First printing: July 1991

Printed in the United States of America

HarperPaperbacks and colophon are trademarks of
HarperCollins*Publishers*

10 9 8 7 6 5 4 3 2 1

DEAD MAN'S RIDE

CHAPTER 1

WHEN THE SHOTS RANG OUT, THE BARBER who was giving Sam Slater a shave almost cut his customer's throat.

Slater lashed out with his left hand and caught the barber's bony wrist in a viselike grip. His ice-blue eyes impaled the trembling man.

"I'm—I'm terrible sorry, mister," stammered the barber, appalled, as he saw blood turn the lather pink beneath Slater's jawbone.

More gunfire erupted in the street. The barber began to quake. Slater plucked the straight razor from the man's paralyzed grasp.

"I think maybe I ought to take over for you."

The barber offered no argument. Released, he backed away from the chair occupied by Slater's

long, lean frame. He was loath to turn his back on
Slater, but curiosity got the better of him, and he
rushed to the door, open to permit what little remained of the spring morning's coolness to infiltrate
the long, narrow room housing his business.

He peered out and down the rutted street, pru-
dent as a deer breaking cover. Townfolk scurried
up and down the boardwalks. A wisp of white gun-
smoke hung in the still air in front of the Farmers
& Merchants Bank. A body lay sprawled in the dust.

Two men on horseback burst out of an alley
across from the bank, shooting up and down the
street. Another pair exploded out of the bank's double doors with such violence that one door came off
its hinges and fell with a shattering of etched glass.
Another horseman galloped around from the back
of the bank, leading two horses. All five men wore
long, white dusters. Their features were concealed
behind bandannas.

The pair emerging from the bank carried bulging gunnysacks which they handed to their mounted
associates before leaping into their own saddles.

"Appears to be a holdup," remarked Slater,
near the barber's shoulder.

The barber jumped. He hadn't heard Slater
Indian-up behind him. Earlier, he had noted the
Apache moccasins on his customer's feet. Unusual
footwear for a white man. With some resentment,
the barber mused that most white men at least had
the courtesy to wear boots and spurs, so that a person might hear them coming.

A hatless, bearded man in overalls stepped out of the mercantile directly across the street from the tonsorial parlor. Standing in the shade of the boardwalk, he brought a double-barreled 10-gauge to bear on the robbers and cut loose, full choke. The buckshot fell well short of the mark, but the roar of the shotgun got the attention of the desperadoes. Two of them returned fire.

The shotgunner staggered. He lowered the 10-gauge and looked in stunned wonder at the blood-leaking holes in the bib of his overalls. Then he pitched forward into the street.

"Oh my God!" strangled the barber, his voice hollow with shock. "They've killed Whitmore."

"He'd have been better off with a rifle," said Slater grimly. "Range was too great for a scattergun."

While he could criticize the merchant's choice of weapons, Slater admired the man's gumption. Seemed like owlhoots bent on cleaning out a frontier bank always underestimated the grit of the locals. There were a lot of men like Whitmore, decent and peace-loving men, who were willing to lay down their lives to protect hard-earned savings from no-account longriders.

The straight razor momentarily forgotten in his left hand, Slater dropped his right to the bone-handled Schofield holstered on his hip. The barber's fleeting hope plunged into disappointment as Slater turned sharply away from the door.

"It's not your fight," carped the barber. "Not

your money they're stealing, or your friends they're shooting."

Slater spun on his heel. A fist of fear squeezed the air out of the barber's lungs as he saw the Schofield materialize in Slater's hand. He didn't see the draw; Slater's hand was quicker than the barber's eye. Slater rolled the gun and offered it butt-first.

"Want to buy in?" he asked harshly. "I'll stake you."

The barber made to reach for the proffered gun. Courage failed him, and the trembling hand dropped to his side.

Holstering the Schofield, Slater gave the man his back.

A coyote yell drew the barber's attention to the street once more. The outlaws were galloping away from the bank, bent low in their saddles, firing left, right, and behind, into the plume of dun-colored dust kicked up by five sets of thundering hooves.

The barber gasped as he realized their flight would bring them past his shop. Petrified, he took root in the doorway. A bullet shattering his plate-glass window returned his senses to him, and he dived for the floor.

Slater was standing beside the chair, facing the pierglass and trying to finish his shave, as the five longriders raced past outside. Another bullet smacked into the pierglass, distorting his image in a spiderweb of cracked fragments.

Frowning, Slater stepped to his right to get an unobstructed view of himself in the mirror and finished scraping two weeks worth of beard bristle from his cheeks.

The rapidly diminishing sound of horses at the hard gallop was immediately replaced by a chorus of shouts, then the clump and clatter of men running on the boardwalks.

The barber picked himself up and hurried across the street to join a quick-gathered crowd of men clustering around Whitmore's body. Slater paused in his work long enough to watch four men lift the corpse and carry it into the mercantile. A half minute later, the wailing lament of a grief-stricken woman sent a fluttering chill down his spine.

Toweling excess lather from the hard brown planes of his cheeks, Slater turned his head slightly to get a good look at the jagged purple scar which ran from his left ear to the corner of his thin-lipped mouth.

He heard someone enter the shop, saw the arrival's reflection in the pierglass, the high-polish shine of the five-pointed star on the man's vest. Slater knew him—Frank Elledge, sheriff of Hanksville, a tall, thin man with curly, black hair, a dense mustache and snapping black eyes.

"Myron said you were still in here." Elledge glanced at the bullet-broken window and mirror. "Too bad you didn't see your way clear to lend a hand."

"See this scar, sheriff? I got it butting into somebody else's business. I like to think I can learn my lessons."

"Damned low-lifes killed two good, decent men," growled Elledge, in a contentious mood.

"It was Black Jack Bohannon and his crew."

"How do you know?"

"Educated guess. Most of the other outlaws in the Devil's Kitchen try not to kill if they can help it. Bohannon and his bunch don't give a damn. Others will aim high on purpose. Bohannon aims for the heart."

Elledge heaved a long breath. "I've got to go after them. Sent a wire to Moab. A posse will enter the Devil's Kitchen from there. Maybe we can catch these bravos between us. I'm forming a posse now. The men here in Hanksville are full of sand, but woefully short on real experience in these matters. That's why I need your help, Slater."

"What makes you think so?"

"You tracked Slick Owens all the way through the Devil's Kitchen, across the Bellfourche to American Fork and back again. You know the lay of the land, and you came out of there in one piece, with Owens belly-down on his horse. That's what makes me think so."

"Don't much care for posses."

"Dammit," growled Elledge. Fists clenched, he took a belligerent step, but stopped short as Slater squared off to face him. Seeing the wisdom in remaining calm and reasonable, the sheriff flexed anger out of his shoulders.

"I know what you aim to do," he said. "Go after Bohannon yourself. You're probably pleased as punch he chose today to ride in here and hit the bank. Gives you a fresh trail. And he's worth—what—$2,000? Four times what we just paid you for the privilege of planting Slick Owens in our local boneyard. The price on Bohannon's head will go up even more now, after this."

"If so, I won't complain."

"You won't complain," echoed Elledge dryly. "You didn't take part in today's activities because you know damned good and well his scalp will be worth more tomorrow. You're one cold-blooded hombre, Slater."

Slater surveyed an array of bottles on the sideboard standing beneath the pierglass. As he splashed astringent smell-pretty on his face, he heard Elledge grunt in disgust and turn for the door.

"Sheriff."

"What?" snapped Elledge.

"I'll ride with you."

Elledge stared a moment, almost asking why and wherefore. He thought better of looking a gift horse in the mouth, and left the barber shop, his stride long with grim purpose.

Slater gave his pierglass reflection a critical once-over. The ghost of a wry smile tugged at the corner of his mouth.

"So you haven't learned your lesson, after all," he murmured.

CHAPTER 2

SLATER WASN'T LONG TAKING THE MEASURE of the Hanksville posse.

The sheriff himself seemed to be savvy enough for the task. He would not permit the others, in their inexperience or anger, to run their horses into the ground. Good thing, too, as none of the other mounts held a candle to Slater's wiry canelo for endurance and speed. The desert mustang was nothing much to look at, and was woefully lacking in social graces, but he was an all-day horse if ever there was one.

Counting Slater and the sheriff, there were seven in the Hanksville posse. One was George Whitmore, the slain merchant's brother. Whitmore's eyes slow-burned with hellfire in a dull and haggard face. He rode bunched over in the saddle like a man gutshot, and constantly swept the far distance with a fevered gaze.

Out in front of the others with Elledge, Slater remarked to the badgetoter that George Whitmore was a definite liability.

"I told him to stay behind," said Elledge, throwing a cautious look over-shoulder, to make certain Whitmore was far enough back to be well out of earshot. "Told him his brother's widow and young son needed him there, worse than we needed him here, but he'd have none of it. Didn't really expect he would."

"One man stone-blind with vengeance can get us all killed."

"It's purely business with you, isn't it?" asked Elledge with hostile exasperation. "No emotion. Nothing wrong with revenge. It burns strong and clean."

"There's no profit in it."

Elledge's dislike for the laconic bounty hunter was as manifest as the outlaw sign they followed east out of Hanksville.

"I can easier understand a man who kills in the heat of passion, than I can one who puts a bullet in another and says 'nothing personal.' But then maybe you never were close enough to anyone to feel a loss so keen you lived for vengeance."

Slater's features were dark and impassive. He spared the lawman a quick and flinty glance, but made no reply. Elledge was trying to nettle him, and

Slater refused to give the sheriff the pleasure of knowing he had succeeded.

Truth was, he *had* suffered personal tragedy, and plenty of it.

As a child he had seen his parents massacred by the Sioux on the Oregon Trail. He had then become the ward of his uncle, a Montana rancher with a strong taste for whiskey. One dark night, his lust and loneliness ignited by a surfeit of rotgut, the uncle had tried to rape his own daughter, Slater's sixteen-year-old cousin. Slater had intervened. The uncle had given him his scar—just before Slater gutted him like a fresh-caught mountain trout.

Self-defense, but Montana called it murder, and Slater fled south, a "papered" man at the tender age of fifteen. South, and straight into Apacheria. Captured by Bedonkohe Chiricahua, the boy had been adopted by the fierce old chieftain, Loco.

Raised by bronco Apaches, Slater had learned from masters the art of hunting and tracking—the very skills he put to such good use as a bounty hunter. In time he came to look on Loco as a true father, and was emotionally hard hit when Loco was murdered by horse soldiers. Murdered—because Loco had laid down his weapons and surrendered to the cavalry in good faith. This foolish trust was repaid with treachery.

Slater narrowly escaped the same fate. Realizing there was no future in living life as an Apache, he had again taken up the ways of the white man.

Finding himself ill-suited to peaceful pursuits, he embarked on a career in manhunting.

As he rode stirrup-to-stirrup with the Hanksville lawman, Slater's mouth quirked at the corners, a cold half-smile. Yes, he knew all about losing loved ones, and the harsh allure of revenge. He had seen the dark side of human nature, in others and in himself. Strangers found him coldly impersonal, and this was so, for Sam Slater had more or less resigned from the human race.

In a way he envied George Whitmore. At least Whitmore could focus his hate on someone specific. Slater wasn't that lucky. He couldn't take the whole Sioux Nation to task for butchering his parents, any more than he could make the entire United States Cavalry answer for the murder of Loco. A man on the edge, he controlled the violence within him with one hard and fast rule. When he let loose the demons in his soul, when he killed, he made sure it was for money, and money alone.

As Elledge had said, purely business. Slater had to keep it that way, for his own sake. He was afraid if he didn't abide by this golden rule the demons within him would take over completely, and he would become worse than the savages who had killed his folks, and the yellow-legs who had hacked Loco to pieces with their sabers.

It amused Slater to think that precious little distinguished him from a ruthless killer like Black Jack Bohannon. Which was exactly why he was best

qualified to bring the notorious outlaw's rampage
to an end.

The Devil's Kitchen was the finest outlaw country Slater had laid eyes on this side of the Sierra
Madre. A high, rough desert etched by wind and
water over the centuries, it provided a maze of canyons and mesas and buttes. Caves and springs were
plentiful. There were arid slopes of red slickrock
and catclaw, and other slopes blanketed with fine
stands of cedar. There were barren alkali flats and
lush meadows hidden deep in box canyons. Water
made all the difference.

Slater had spent weeks hunting Slick Owens in
this country. He knew that water was in abundant
supply; the trick was knowing where to find it. Or
half the trick, anyway. Some springs were sweet-
water, while others were impregnated with gypsum,
sometimes emitting a stench of sulfide so strong it
could be smelled a quarter-mile downwind.

The water was there, but you couldn't always
count on it. He had heard tell of one spring, nor-
mally good drinking, which could turn deadly poi-
sonous on any given day.

The posse passed through blue clay hills and
across a sagebrush flat rippling with blow sand.
Next came a stretch of sand dunes, stacked up by
the prevailing westerly winds against the cliffs
known locally as the Sunset Rim. The tracks of the
outlaw gang were clear in the white sand.

The Sunset Rim was the western edge of the

Devil's Kitchen, forty north-south miles of cap rock. Dozens of canyons pierced the face of the Rim. Some dead-ended; others led into the heart of the Devil's Kitchen.

As they walked their tired horses through the last of the dunes, the sun hammered at their backs, plummeting toward the edge of the purple desert behind them. The dying day's light stressed the ribbons of color in the face of the escarpment before them: plum red, burnt orange, pale yellow, and creamy white.

Slater gave Black Jack Bohannon credit for a job well-planned. The outlaw leader had hit the Farmers & Merchants Bank at midday, knowing a posse would be hard on his heels, and timing it so that nightfall would find him and his gang reaching the Devil's Kitchen. Bohannon knew the canyons like the back of his hand. He could travel them in the quarter-moon darkness with ease. The same could not necessarily be said for his pursuers.

They came upon five horses in a grove of scrub cedar hard by a rocky draw. The draw branched off a deep rincon emerging from a narrow gorge where the blue shadows of night had already gathered.

"I was afraid of this," muttered Elledge sourly as they watched the five spent horses grazing on the far side of the draw. "Reckon we'll find six sets of tracks now. Someone was waiting here with fresh horses."

"That's Bohannon's way," said Slater.

"Yeah. They switched their tack over as fast as

any Pony Express rider ever did, and were on their way before you could whistle Dixie."

"They sure run the finish off those ponies," commented a young man named Bryner, a range rider employed by the T Anchor Ranch who had happened into Hanksville in time to volunteer for the posse.

"Damned outlaws always have the best horse-flesh in the territory," groused Whitmore.

"Well, I should say so," said Bryner glibly. "They rustle all the race mares and blooded stock they can find."

"And they take special care of them, too," chimed in Ricker, Hanksville's burly blacksmith. "Spend a lot of time caring for their ponies. Keep 'em in the best graze and take 'em any distance they have to in order to get 'em watered regular. Lot of the hardscrabble ranchers in and abouts the Kitchen supply them with oats, so's they can grain their horses every day. A gallon of oats every day, along with desert grasses, will put a right fine finish on a horse."

"Can't blame the ranchers," said Elledge. "They figure it's better to keep on the good side of pilgrims like Bohannon."

"Looks like they left their dusters piled up under that tree yonder," observed Stoddard, the Hanksville gunsmith.

"They don't need them anymore," said Slater. "They wore them during the robbery so they wouldn't accidentally shoot each other in the fracas. A quick way to tell friend from foe."

"We're burning daylight," growled Whitmore. "Those bastards killed my brother and a bank teller, and they've got $12,000 that belongs to us, and we're sitting here shooting the breeze."

"Our horses are almost bottomed out, George," said Elledge. "We're not going to outrun them. We'll just have to follow their sign and hope we don't lose the scent." He glanced sidelong at Slater. "Fortunately, we have a man here who can track an ant across a boulder field."

"So what do we do now?" asked Ricker, wincing as he shifted stiffly in the saddle.

"There's a seep a half-mile south," said Slater. "Good a place as any to night. We'll pick up the trail at first light."

"And ride into the valley of the shadow," murmured Bryner, a trace of apprehension in his voice as he scanned the forbidding heights which marked the western rim of the Devil's Kitchen.

"I say we keep on," said Whitmore, obstreperous. "They might ride all night."

"We're not taking a vote," snapped Elledge tersely. "And we're not going to run our horses 'til they drop. I for one don't fancy being put afoot deep in those canyons. Lead the way, Slater."

Slater angled the cat-footed canelo down into the draw and turned south.

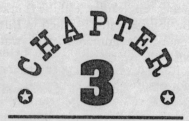

CHAPTER 3

THE SEEP TRICKLED OUT OF A FISSURE IN THE Sunset Rim, to gather in a rock basin at the edge of the dunes. The posse camped in the brush-rimmed *hueco*, putting their horses on a stake rope weighted down with large stones. Slater kept apart from the others, beyond the reach of the fire's flickering amber light.

He pondered the little ironies life was prone to throw in his path. Here he was, a wanted man himself, riding with a posse of law-abiders. Of course, none of these men knew he was on the dodge. It was a long way from Montana. Still, he felt a trifle ill at ease.

Coyotes serenaded in the high lonesome, and the sweet scent of night-blooming sand puffs drifted on the evening breeze from the whispering dunes. The fire crackled cheerfully, and the Hanksville men talked in low tones. Slater listened to Elledge hand out night-guard assignments, and watched the lanky sheriff walk over.

Sitting on his heels, Elledge tossed a thumb over his shoulder. "Got some java cooking, if you want some."

"No thanks."

"Not very sociable, are you?"

"Not very."

Elledge consulted the star-bright sky. "George Whitmore doesn't much cater to the idea of your being along on this ride."

"That so."

"Has to do with the reward money. He figures it ought to go to his brother's widow. He's got all the others to agree, in principle. All except Johnny McVey, that is."

Slater let his gaze stray away from Elledge. McVey sat on the opposite side of the rock tank. Firelight glimmered off the conchos on his hatband, and off the big-roweled spurs strapped to his boots. He was meticulously, lovingly, cleaning his pistols, a matched set of Colt Lightning Models.

"What do you know about McVey?" asked Slater.

"He's worked for most of the outfits hereabouts. Never stays long with any one of them. Got a hot temper. Fancies himself a gun artist. Talks a good game, but he hasn't seen enough winters to have done all he claims. He gets to strutting like a bantam rooster sometimes, trying to pick fights with the other cowboys, and the ranchers eventually have to hogleg him to keep the peace."

Slater nodded. He had already pegged McVey; had crossed paths with many like him. Barely old enough to require whisker-scraping, they wore big guns tied low, swaggered and bragged and usually died young in search of a glorious reputation. As a rule they were unpredictable, sometimes dangerous.

"So what about the reward money?" pressed Elledge.

"What about it?"

"Any objections to giving it to Mattie Whitmore if we catch Bohannon and his bunch?"

"You won't."

Elledge frowned. "That's a helluva thing to say."

Slater stretched out on his blanket, resting his head in the dip of his saddle, and tugged his hat down over his eyes.

"Then why did you come with us, if you didn't think we'd catch them?" asked Elledge.

"I was coming this way anyhow."

"We may surprise you," said the sheriff, affronted. "Most of these men have ridden in a posse or two before."

"I'm sure. Posses are the favorite pastime of local merchants and small-change farmers. Breaks the monotony. But when the going gets rough they generally spook. I'm not telling you anything you don't know, sheriff, so don't bother saying it ain't so."

Elledge grimaced. "This time's different. Two men are dead."

"Good intentions won't make the grade. Your posse will start worrying more about the living than the dead when the lead starts getting slung. Except Whitmore. He'll probably just get himself killed, and maybe one or two of the others."

"So you figure we'll turn back with tails tucked, and you'll go on alone and collect the bounty for yourself."

"Could very well turn out that way. Until then I don't have to keep my eyes peeled for a trigger-happy posse."

Elledge rose and walked away, his movements crisp and angry.

Slater wondered why he hadn't told Elledge the real reason he had come along. Fact was, he figured he might be able to keep some of these good, decent men alive long enough to see Hanksville again.

He rested his left hand on the Spencer carbine lying next to him, and drifted off to sleep, only to wake to the sound of an angel singing hymns.

The spring wagon, pulled by a team of mules, had a canvas cover on a box frame. The man working the reins was old and bent, wearing thick spectacles and a dusty black frock coat. But for wings of bristly gray hair above his ears, he was bald, and he looked plenty old enough to be the father of the woman who sat beside him. Maybe even the grand-father.

The man hauled back on the leathers when he saw Slater and the others emerge from the brush rimming the *hueco*. The woman stopped singing "Amazing Grace." She had a fine voice, thought Slater. Clear as a bell on Sunday morning.

"What in tarnal creation . . ." breathed Elledge.

Slater moved toward the wagon. Ordering the others to lay back, Elledge fell into step alongside. When he saw the badge on the sheriff's vest, the man in the wagon lifted his hands toward heaven and let go a lusty "Praise the Lord!" that echoed off the cap rock in the still morning air. The mules felt the give in the reins and moved. They were past ready to get to the water in the rock tank. The spring wagon lurched forward, and the man was very nearly pitched out of his seat. Slater stepped in to latch onto the cheekstrap and collar of the offside mule, halting the team.

"What are you folks doing out here?" asked Elledge.

"Spreading the gospel, sheriff. Spreading the gospel. I am the Reverend Joshua Hazen, brother, and this is Sister Rachel."

Slater took a closer look at the woman. She wore a severely plain, high-collared dress of brown serge. Tendrils of hair escaped from beneath her bonnet. The hair was a rich chestnut color, with fire-red highlights compliments of the early sun. She was strikingly beautiful and Slater stared without meaning to. She held a hymnal with both hands and lifted it as though to shield herself from his brash gaze.

"It ain't safe for you folks out in this neck of the woods," said Elledge, stroking his unruly mustache. "This is outlaw country."

"Yes, we know," said the preacher, with an embarrassed smile. "In fact, I thought for a moment you men were outlaws yourselves. But I fear no evil. The Lord is with me."

Slater wondered just how strong the man's faith really was. He had looked mighty anxious a moment ago.

"Take my advice, you'll head west," said Elledge. "I reckon a lot of souls in the Devil's Kitchen need saving something fierce, but I sure as . . . I sure wouldn't try doing it."

"But that is my calling, sheriff. 'Go ye therefore and teach all nations, baptizing them in the name of the Father, and of the Son, and of the Holy Ghost. Teaching them to observe all things whatsoever I have commanded you.' St. Matthew, chapter 28. Sinners and salvation, brother. For months now, Sister Rachel and I have traveled the frontier shining the saving light of the Master's all-forgiving love on those who languish in darkness. I will exalt the name of the Lord God Almighty among the iniquitous."

"I just hope they don't exalt you from the nearest tree," muttered Elledge.

The preacher beamed at Slater. "Have you been saved, son?"

"Not hardly. My folks were Godfearing, though. My mother used to read to me from the Good Book. I still remember bits and pieces. Something about 'beware of false prophets, which come to you in sheep's clothing, but inwardly they are wolves.' The Book of James, chapter 7."

The preacher nodded vigorously. "Yes, yes. Well, if you gentlemen would consent to sharing your waterhole, we'll be on our way."

Slater let go of the mule's harness and Elledge made a curt go-ahead-and-kill-yourself gesture. They watched the wagon trundle on toward the *hueco*. The sheriff tossed a puzzled glance Slater's way.

"Book of James? Ain't no such."

Smiling faintly, Slater peered intently after the wagon. "You know it, and I know it. Kind of strange that a preacher didn't, wouldn't you say?"

"Maybe he was just being polite not bringing up your mistake."

"I doubt that. Never met a Bible thumper who wasn't quick to show how much he knew scripture."

"You mean to tell me . . ."

"Said what I mean. Wolves in sheep's clothing. That preacher man may have traveled months across the frontier, but it wasn't by wagon. He doesn't know the next thing about handling a team. And that woman . . ." Slater shook his head. "I swear

I've seen her somewhere before. Just can't place it. But I know it wasn't at some riverside revival."

"Maybe I should *pasear* on over there and have another talk with the good preacher."

"Why bother? It's Bohannon and his gang we want to talk to. Let's get saddled up and go find us some of those souls you were talking about."

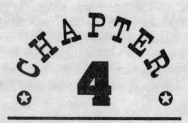

CHAPTER 4

A FEW MILES INTO THE GORGE, SLATER stopped the posse and dismounted to look closer at the ground. He walked fifty yards ahead and then back, going down on one knee now and again to read the story told by imprints in the patches of dirt and sand trapped in rock depressions.

Elledge and the posse stayed mounted. All but the sheriff kept a wary eye on the rimrock high overhead. Elledge watched the bounty hunter at work.

"One of their horses has come up lame," said Slater finally. "Favoring the right foreleg. Could be an abscess under the shoe. The rider's walking the horse. The rest pushed on."

"The one afoot might hold back somewhere and lay up for us," said the Hanksville lawman.

"Might." Slater didn't sound concerned. He climbed aboard the canelo, glanced back at the posse, then at Elledge. "Sheriff, it's time you sent these men home. Better yet, take them yourself. Leave Bohannon and his wild bunch to me."

Elledge bristled. "Oh, I see. You don't need us. You can handle these owlhoots all by your lonesome."

"I'll have a better chance without you than I would with you."

Whitmore gut-kicked his horse and came closer, having overheard Elledge's loud and angry retort, and putting two and two together.

"Sheriff, you can't do it. Who's to say he won't keep the $12,000 taken from the bank for himself? I don't trust him and you shouldn't, either."

Elledge, watching the bounty hunter for reaction, became very concerned for Whitmore's well-being.

"Keep your trap shut, George," he advised.

Slater's smile was cold as ice. "Don't worry, sheriff. I only kill for money." He looked Whitmore over with all the emotion of an undertaker measuring a client for a pine box. Then he turned the canelo and started up the canyon.

A mile farther on, the canyon forked. The outlaw sign led them up the left branch. This turned out to be a dead end. A trail angled up a slope strewn with boulders and choked with brush.

"Too bad we can't just sprout wings and fly," murmured Bryner, a rueful smile playing across his face as he craned his neck to follow the rise of the trail.

"You might 'fore we're done," rumbled Ricker apprehensively. "Wings, and strummin' on a harp, in the bargain, iffen there's one of them yeggs hidden up yonder, waitin' on us to get halfway."

Bryner gave the burly blacksmith a funny look. "You sure have a comforting way with words."

"We'll have to walk our horses up," Slater told them. "Move as fast as you can and keep well apart."

They began the climb. Slater took the lead. The trail snaked over and around steep pitches of naked sandstone. Their horses slipped and stumbled on red slickrock, losing hide, and the stench of burnt hooves was strong.

Slater climbed hard and made good time. He had the lungs and the legs for it. The canelo was a mountain mustang by birth, and gave him no trouble. The other men were less fortunate. They were flatlanders, and did not ascend the trail with Slater's confidence. Their horses, sensing their fear, balked and braced. Slater wrote it off as a small miracle that all the men and all the mounts reached the rim in one piece.

Topping out on a narrow gravel point, they turned east along the skyline to tableland gently sloped and covered with catclaw, what the Utes called *wee-ump*, also known as barberry. Profuse yellow flowers perfumed the cooling high-country breeze that dried the sweat on men and horses.

The tableland dipped into a drainage draw, and

the draw took them north into a cedar-rimmed swale. Leaving the swale, they crossed a hogback of slickrock. Here they found trails cut four to six inches deep into solid rock. For centuries game had crossed this rocky backbone in search of graze and water. Reaching the crest, Slater looked down the other side and saw why. A valley lay before him, nestled between tree-cloaked ridges. A creek danced through a bottomland lush with bluestem. Scattered cattle grazed. A mile away, at the far end of the hidden valley, a house, barn and corral stood in the shade of tall cottonwoods.

"Could that be Bohannon's hideout?" asked Elledge.

Slater shook his head. "Belongs to a small-time rancher named Swope. Runs a few cattle. Came across him when I was hunting Slick Owens. Bohannon may sit at his table now and then, but he wouldn't hole up here."

"Got no use for a man who trucks with thieves and murderers," muttered Whitmore.

"So much for Christian tolerance," said Elledge.

"Men like Swope don't have a choice," said Slater. "They're caught between a rock and a hard place. They're better off staying friendly with Bohannon and his kind. Much healthier that way. The outlaws rule the Devil's Kitchen, not the law."

"Lie down with dogs, you get up with fleas," snapped Whitmore.

Elledge sighed. "Let's ride."

"Sure," said Slater. "But let's ride slow and spread out."

"You said Bohannon wouldn't be here."

"They've got one man on foot, remember? He's fallen behind the others, and we're not too far behind him. He's had a long, hard walk. Could be he's partaking of Swope's hospitality."

They rode up the valley well apart and watchful. Slater saw no activity at the ranch until they were a holler away. Then a man emerged from the house, pausing in the porch shade, hefting a shotgun. Slater was aware of McVey dragging his rifle from his saddle boot, and cursed under his breath. The man on the porch wisely leaned the shotgun against the house and stepped out into sunlight to wave and call howdy. Slater reined the canelo sharply and quartered over to McVey.

"Leather that long gun," he said. "It's Swope."

"You're better off not telling me what to do," said McVey.

"Right. And you're better off doing what I tell you."

McVey defiantly held Slater's ice-blue gaze for a long time. Then he snorted disdain and booted the rifle. Slater angled away, thinking that McVey was a powderkeg waiting for a match.

Swope was a bent-backed, rickety man, rail-thin and scraggly-bearded. A quid of tobacco pouched his cheek. Slater checked the canelo and dismounted, scanning the house windows and the open doors of the barn. Between house and barn was a corral, hosting a couple of horses.

Sheriff Elledge stepped down too. The rest of the posse stayed in their saddles. Slater shook his head. He was going to have the devil's own time keeping these amateurs alive. The fools sat their horses like tin cans on fence posts, waiting for a potshot.

"Howdy, sheriff," said Swope.

"We're after Bohannon and his bunch. Held up the Hanksville bank yesterday. Killed two men. Seen 'em?"

"Sure I seen 'em," answered Swope, throwing a sly, sidelong glance at Slater. He recognized the bounty man, and figured that if Slater was on Bohannon's trail, then the sheriff already knew the answer to his question. "Them gallop-and-gunshot boys been through here. But then you know that, don't you?"

Slater smiled faintly. Swope was a survivor. He knew better than to take sides. A man in the middle, smack dab between the law and the lawless, he knew he had to play both ends.

"How many?" asked the Hanksville badgetoter.

"Five riders, an hour after 'can see.' They watered their horses, had a cup of coffee, moved on. Went north. Couple hours ago another came, leading a lame horse. He swapped for one of mine, lit out after the others."

"Know any of 'em?"

Swope chewed a moment, squinting at Elledge, then spat a stream of brown juice.

"Knowed Black Jack and his brother Clyde. Never seen the rest before, and they didn't bother introducin' themselves."

Slater figured Swope was lying about that, but didn't hold it against him.

"Step down, boys, and come inside," offered Swope. "I've got coffee and biscuits. . . ."

Whitmore dismounted and lurched forward to confront Swope, his chin jutting belligerently.

"You sorry ole cuss. You expect me to drink from the same cup as the man who shot my brother down in cold blood?"

Swope stood his ground, utterly impassive. "Were you in my boots, you wouldn't be so quick with the high and mighty airs, mister. You ain't got them jaspers for neighbors, like I have. What do you want I should do? Pull up stakes? Not on your life. This valley's mine. Signed and sealed. Has been nigh on ten year. Best graze in the Devil's Kitchen. Hell, in most of these parts a cow has to have a mouth six feet wide and graze at a gallop to get enough to eat. But not in this valley. I won't easy give it up. I. . . ."

The canelo ground-hitched, Slater was heading for the corral, and this distracted Swope. He hastened after the bounty hunter. The sheriff followed suit.

One of the two horses in the corral was a sway-backed nag. Slater figured this one had to belong to

Swope. The other was a tall blaze sorrel, favoring its right foreleg. Slipping between cedar posts into the corral, he picked up a bucket and sniffed its contents.

"What is it?" asked Elledge.

"Turpentine and wintergreen. Horse has an abscess, you soak its hoof in this for a spell." Spotting something else, Slater put the bucket down and plucked a cigarette butt from the hardpack. He sniffed it, too. The pungent smell of burnt tobacco was still strong. He looked sharply at Swope. The rancher appeared nervous. He struck Slater as a man who had something to hide.

"I was thinking," said Slater casually, flicking the spent quirly away and hunkering down to examine the hardpack more closely, "that a particular outlaw might be real fond of that apron-faced sorrel over there. After all, he hauled the critter up a mountainside when he could have easier left it in the canyon and not gone to the bother."

"What are you getting at?" asked the sheriff.

Slater shrugged. "I see rowel marks here. You don't wear gut-hooks, do you, Swope?"

"I said they been here. Been here and gone."

"Gone? All of 'em? That cigarette was just smoked. As I recall, you don't use tobacco."

Swope gave the game away then; Slater saw the man's eyes flick toward the barn. He looked, too, saw the glint of sunlight from up in the hayloft. His warning yell coincided with the gunshot. He saw Elledge spin and fall, and heard the sheriff gasp as the bullet struck.

CHAPTER 5

UNDER THE GUN, CAUGHT OUT IN THE OPEN, many men would freeze—an often fatal mistake. Slater knew better. He moved, and moved fast. Drawing the Schofield, he fired three times on the run, quartering across the corral and heading for the barn's side door. A horse screamed, men shouted, more shots were fired. Swope's broomtail, wall-eyed, galloped a dust-raising circle around the corral; Slater had to feint and dodge to keep from getting run over. He put his back against the wall by the side door. Now out of the bushwhacker's sight, he paused to throw a quick look across the corral, wondering how the others fared.

The sheriff was down and unmoving. Swope was running for the house. Rifle in hand, Whitmore was running toward the barn. As the two men passed, Whitmore slammed the stock of his rifle into Swope's face. Swope went down like fresh-cut timber. Whitmore threw a hasty shot at the hayloft and kept running. Slater shook his head in wonder. Sheriff Elledge had said there was nothing wrong with revenge, that it burned pure and clean. In Slater's opinion, revenge made fools out of rational men, and corpses out of fools.

Behind Whitmore, Bryner and McVey were also slinging lead at the barn. Both men were off their horses and looking for cover. The blacksmith, Ricker, was having trouble getting boot out of stirrup; his horse was fiddlefooting and Ricker kept hopping around. Stoddard, the gunsmith, had lost control of his horse. The cayuse was galloping away with an occasional crowhopping kick and Stoddard was running after it. The scene was comic—had the situation been less dangerous Slater might have laughed. The gunsmith belatedly realized he could not outrun a horse, and dived for cover behind the nearest cottonwood.

Slater took an extra half minute to reload. He had learned from experience that it was a wise man who filled his guns if an opportunity presented itself. Half-cocking the Schofield, he pulled the barrel latch, and the barrel dropped. The cylinder swung up and the C.A. King shell extractor kicked out the empties. He plucked three new loads out of his belt and thumbed these into the empty chambers. This done, he closed the gun, lowering the hammer to lock the frame.

Whitmore earned a faceful of splinters as an outlaw bullet smacked into a cedar post; he dropped flat on the ground beside the corral fence. McVey and Bryner were still shooting it up. Slater entertained little hope they would hit anything. Bryner was a cowhand. He had probably used his thumbbuster more often for driving nails than he had for shooting. And McVey? Slater pegged him as a kid long on brag and short on real experience. The type who could put a hole in a silver dollar on the fly, but who suffered from "buck fever" in situations like this.

Which left it up to Slater. That suited him fine. He just hoped to avoid a stray bullet long enough to get the job done—the so-called posse was throwing a lot of strays around.

Pulling the latch string, he threw the side door open and entered the barn. There were empty stalls left and right. Straight ahead was the carriageway, partially filled by the bulk of a dilapidated buckboard.

Slater ventured out into the carriageway, training gaze and gunbarrel up and to the right, in the direction of the hayloft. He didn't have time to fire a shot, much less get an image of the man he stalked clearly imprinted on his mind. He saw muzzle-flash and heard the bullet slap into the wood of a stall behind him. As he rolled under the buckboard, another bullet splintered the warped and weathered bed boards and plunked into the ground not nearly far enough away to suit him.

He kept rolling, out from under the wagon, got off a shot, but the outlaw was on the move, and Slater missed. A bullet glanced off the iron of a wheel rim and shimmied away. Slater rolled back under the buckboard.

Entering the barn without knowing the layout had been a risk; now he considered his situation and found it wanting. The loft was just an upper platform built of cedar poles across the front part of the barn. It did not extend all around. Its doors, directly above the main barn doors, gave the outlaw an excellent vantage point from which he could keep Whitmore and the others pinned down.

Slater saw the ladder, and knew immediately that it was out of the question. If he wasn't gunned down trying to reach it, he surely would be if he tried to climb it. And now he was pinned down, too, huddling beneath the buckboard in straw and dung, waiting for the longrider to turn the wagon into kindling. The man had more than one gun. Slater heard the distinctive bark of a repeating rifle as the outlaw fired a few rounds into the buckboard.

"Enough is enough," muttered Slater.

Holstering the Schofield, he dug in and pushed against the buckboard's front axle. As he had hoped, the wagon was not too heavy for him to move. He put his back into it. The buckboard began to roll backwards, in the direction of the barn doors. The outlaw fired several more times, but Slater was crouched at the front of the wagon, and the longrider was shooting down into the bed.

When the buckboard was directly beneath the loft, Slater rolled out and, flat on his back, sent five slugs straight up through the floor of the loft, aiming between the poles and spaced well apart.

Reloading, he listened hard. A pole creaked beneath the outlaw's weight. Straw drifted down.

"Better throw your guns down," advised Slater, getting to his feet. "Give it up."

"Go to hell," was the gruff reply, followed by two shots fired down through the floor. The outlaw was homing in on Slater's voice, but the bounty hunter had already moved.

Slater fired twice more, then paused. He saw the poles bend beneath the man's weight and sent three more rounds up into the hayloft. The outlaw cried out, stumbled, and pitched off the edge of the hayloft, landing in the carriageway.

With one bean left in the cylinder, Slater moved in with all due caution. The outlaw lay spread-eagle on his back. A Henry repeater lay beside him. Slater kicked the rifle away. A closer look convinced him this precaution was unnecessary. The man was dead. The bullet had entered at a sharp upward angle near the sternum and, ripping into the lungs or heart, killed instantly.

Hearing footsteps, Slater looked around to see Whitmore framed in the doorway.

"Kill him?"

"Lucky shot," said Slater.

"Who is it?"

"Don't know."

McVey slipped past Whitmore to sit on his heels and look the dead man over. He held a Colt Lightning in each hand. The guns dangled between his knees.

"Looks like a breed," he said.

Slater had come to the same conclusion, based on the outlaw's long, lank, black hair and dark, broad features.

Whitmore came closer. "Wonder if this is the one killed my brother?"

Reloading the Schofield through force of habit, Slater shrugged. Whitmore hawked and spat on the dead man. Slater turned on his heel and left the barn.

Bryner and Stoddard were bending over the sheriff. Slater joined them, and in a glance knew that Elledge was gone beaver.

Elledge knew it. He experienced an odd, numbing cold spreading from his extremities, moving up his arms and legs. He knew, somehow, that when the cold reached his chest, his heart, he would be dead. Already his vision was beginning to fail him; he could barely make Slater out through blotches of fuzzy blackness.

"Slater," he whispered, too weak almost to speak. "Slater . . . you take over . . . lead posse. . . ."

"I'll pass."

"Stoddard, you . . ." Elledge went rigid, sucked

in air, and as he breathed out slowly and for the final time he said, "I'm finished. . . ."

Stunned, Stoddard rocked back on his heels and sat down hard. "Sheriff's dead," he said, sounding lost and bewildered.

"This one ain't," announced Ricker, bending over Swope. "But his face is ruint, that's for sure and certain."

Only Stoddard's horse had wandered far. The other mounts stood in the speckled shade of the cottonwoods. Whitmore went to his, his stride quickened with hot anger, and when he came back to them a coiled rope was clenched in his hand.

"I say we hang the sorry cuss," he growled.

"What?" Ricker stood up and stepped hastily away from Swope, staring at the unconscious man like he had never seen Swope before.

"You heard me. I say hang him high. He as much as killed the sheriff, even if he wasn't the one to pull the trigger. He knew that son of a bitch was hid out in the barn. I didn't hear him warning anybody."

Slater stood. "He'd been the one warned. He knew he'd get the first bullet were he to sell the half-breed down the river."

"You don't know that!" yelled Whitmore, his face mottled with congesting blood, his eyes hard with hate. "In my book, he's as bad as Bohannon and his bunch. Long as men like this harbor long-riders we'll never be rid of the vermin. I say we set an example."

Bryner looked hopefully to Stoddard. "Mister, the sheriff put you in charge. What do you say?"

Stoddard was staring at Elledge's blood-soaked shirt front, and for the first time Slater realized the sheriff and the gunsmith had been friends.

"I say why the hell not? Whitmore's probably right."

"It ain't proper, hanging a man from a cottonwood," said Bryner, by way of protest. "Branches are too limber. I seen a rustler hanged from a cottonwood. He bobbed up and down like . . . like a . . . well, I dunno what like, but I know it weren't a pretty sight. It don't break his neck, you see. This rustler, he just danced and kicked and made funny noises. His tongue got all swole and stuck out of his mouth. His eyes liked to popped out of his head. I swear, before he died his neck was stretched ten inches, be my guess. Maybe more. One of the awfulest things I ever seen."

"I'm going to hang this sorry cuss," said Whitmore fiercely. "I'll do the job alone, if I must." He started for Swope.

Slater moved to intercept him. "You're not going to do it at all."

Whitmore squared off. The rifle in his right hand came up, and Slater's hand dropped to the butt of the holstered Schofield. A part of him said this wasn't his concern—a harsh, brutal part forged in the crucible of long years spent in the uncivilized business of manhunting. But a spark of conscience prodded him into action. None of the others—these so-called honest, decent, law-abiding men—were going to stand up against Whitmore. Revenge burned so hot and bright in him that the others could not help but cringe away from its heat.

Slater never knew if it was Stoddard or Bryner who pistol-whipped him. He carelessly turned his back on both as he faced Whitmore. Suddenly he was falling, his head exploding with a blinding pain. He braced for impact with the ground. The impact never came, as far as he could tell. He simply kept falling, falling, falling into a black and bottomless pit.

CHAPTER 6

MATTIE OGHAM LEAFED RAPTUROUSLY through the dog-eared pages of an old Montgomery Ward catalogue, marveling at ladies fashions the likes of which she had never seen before. Her toes digging in the dust at the bottom of the porch steps, she dreamed a young woman's dreams. She imagined her gingham dress, hardly more than a tattered rag in spite of countless mendings, magically transformed into an elegant gown of the finest satin and lace. Her hair, the color of cornsilk, hung long, unkempt and dirty, yet she imagined it clean and textured like silk, catching the light of crystal chandeliers and done up in a stylish, perfumed coiffure with diamond pins.

Her father shuffled out of the cabin, yawning

away the last vestige of his traditional midday siesta. Blunt, black-nailed fingers fumbled with the fastenings as Pop Ogham tried to attach suspenders to trousers. Squinting critically at the sun-hammered, scrub-cloaked bluffs encircling the basin he called home, he scratched without much vigor at graybacks setting up house beneath his sun-faded, pink longjohns. Then he noticed the girl sitting spraddlelegged on the porch steps and grimaced.

"Mattie! Put that dang-blasted book away! I swear, child. You'll dream your life away."

She was petulant. "Not much else to do in this Godforsaken hole."

"You could go fetch your pa some water out of that thar trough, dammit. It's hotter'n a whore's private parts today."

"Fetch your own water," said Mattie.

"Don't talk back to me, child!" roared Ogham, swaying as he felt the effect of the snakehead he had put away that morning. "I've half a mind to burn that dang-blasted wishbook of yours. Better yet, I'll keep it in the crapper and use it page by page to . . ."

She shot to her feet and turned on him with such vehemence that Ogham flinched, stumbling backward against the door frame. The catalogue was clutched tightly against her breast. She was a right pretty thing, he reflected. Reminded him of her mother, rest her soul, with that small, round mouth and pert, turned-up nose and the pale blue eyes that turned smoke-gray when she got riled—like now.

And like her mother, Mattie could be a holy terror when her dander was up.

"Just try it!" she screamed. "You just try it, you old drunk. I'll pizen your likker. See if I don't."

Ogham didn't doubt it for a second. A stomach full of wolf-bait strychnine—was there a worse way to die?

"Hell, child," he grumbled, resentfully wondering why, on top of all his other tribulations, he had to be burdened with a hellcat for a daughter. "Keep your dang-blasted book. You can dream all you want. You ain't never gonna have any of those purty gewgaws."

"Yes I will!" she cried, almost in tears. "Yes I will, you'll see. Jack says he gonna take me to Denver and San Francisco. He says he's gonna buy me seven dresses, one for each day of the week. He says we'll eat at the fanciest restaurants, and ride in a carriage with velvet seats, and stay at hotels where. . . ."

Ogham flapped a hand at her and walked away. "Jack says! Jack Bohannon and the truth ain't even related. He'd promise you the moon, iffen he knew a way to steal it out of the sky."

"Jack and I are engaged," she snapped.

Ogham laughed, a cold and brittle sound. "Engaged? Child, Black Jack Bohannon is engaged to half the girls in the territory. The only reason he ain't engaged to the other half is 'cause he just ain't had the time yet to get around to it."

This left Mattie speechless with rage. Satisfied,

Pop Ogham left her in the porch shade and trudged across the hardpack, wincing at the bright heat of the midday sun. Fifty paces north of the cabin was a limestone bench, on the southern flank of a sandy ridge thick with brush. A spring trickled out of the limestone, and a sluice had been built to channel the water into a long trough. This work was not Ogham's; he wasn't that industrious. Six years ago he had found this place abandoned, and moved right in, lock, stock and whiskey bottle.

From this base he rustled horses, sometimes cattle, from the ranches west of the Devil's Kitchen. The cattle were trailed north to Colorado mine-fields, where top dollar was paid for beef on the hoof. It was a profession that could be as lucrative as it was dangerous, and Ogham was an old hand at the game, but he seldom had two coins to rub to-gether. He had a bad habit of losing his ill-gotten gains to goldfield gamblers.

In his younger days he had done his thieving alone. Now he used helpers, three or four young-sters recruited from the dirt-poor pioneer families ignorant enough to try and eke out a living in the Devil's Kitchen.

The horses he sold to outlaws, who generally re-spected Ogham as the purveyor of the best re-mounts they could get. As a rewrite man, Pop had no peer. Brand altering was his only talent, aside from the ability to consume prodigious quantities of raw liquor. He was an artist with the running iron, and he had introduced the technique of "skinning out a brand" to the area. No one could better Ogham when it came to cutting out the patch of hide that carried the brand and sewing up the sides with a strip of whang leather. When the stitching was removed a couple of months later, Ogham used the scar as part of the new brand.

Pop had been "a little on the rustle" for most of his adult life, and he had never been caught. In his better days, he would have sensed the men who watched him from the brush up on the ridge. But as he dunked his head into the trough, he was completely unaware that he had company.

Watching like vultures, they sat their lathered horses a hundred yards away—four men, hardcases from hat to heel, bristling with weapons.

"Looks like Pop is hymn-singing drunk again," observed Bill Lukan.

"Ain't he always?" grinned Bill's brother, Bob.

"Place looks okay," said Bill.

"Shuddup," sighed Clyde Bohannon. The Lukan brothers were forever jabbering like bluejays. In itself, that was bad enough. Worse, they never said anything important. They would waste their breath and everyone else's time pointing out the obvious, or mentioning things everybody already knew. They weren't very bright, mused Clyde. In their linsey shirts and woolen trousers and wideawake hats, they looked like hayseeds straight off the farm. Both were blond and blue-eyed; their folks had been Swedish emigrants. Despite their ap-

pearance, Clyde knew them as killers without conscience.

"There's Pop's girl," Bill said and grinned.

"Ain't she purty?" Bob grinned.

"Makes your palms sweat to look on her," said
Bob.

"She's Jack's girl," reminded the fourth horseman. "You'd be wise to keep your paws off her, both
of you."

Clyde threw a sidelong glance at the fourth man.
His name was Shad Mowry, or so he said. Clyde had
a strong hunch Mowry wasn't trying to protect Black
Jack's property. In fact, he'd shown a strong interest in Mattie Ogham himself. It was just a matter of
time before Mowry and Jack butted heads over the
girl.

A full black beard made Mowry look older than
his years. Hooded eyes were as flat and lifeless as
a doll's. He kept strictly to himself. He never got
drunk and rowdy. Never got angry. He seldom
spoke, and never talked about his past. He was as
taciturn as the Lukan brothers were talkative.
Mowry was a hard man to like, and Clyde hadn't
tried. Jack had him along because he didn't seem
to have a nerve in his body, and because he was a
crack shot with his Remington Army sidegun and
the Winchester Yellow Boy in his saddle boot. What
his brother Jack wanted was fine by Clyde. He
didn't mind playing the role of the gang's second fid-
dle.

"We know Jack's got his brand on her," said Bill.

"Yeah, we know that," said Bob.

"It don't hurt to talk, long as we don't touch," said Bill.

"Stow the noise," rasped Clyde.

The sound of a rider coming through the brush on the rim behind them turned everyone's attention away from the Ogham place, except Mowry's. His unblinking gaze remained fastened on Mattie Ogham.

Black Jack Bohannon stopped his horse between Clyde and the Lukans. He was bigger than the twins put together. His shoulders were as brawny as a bull buffalo's, his thighs as thick as tree trunks. His lantern-jawed face was craggy and pitted. Unlike his dour brother Clyde, Jack maintained an I-don't-give-a-damn attitude about life—his or anyone else's. Jack was a grinner. Even when he was killing, he kept on grinning.

"Boys," said Jack, "how you all have come so far on the owlhoot trail I'll never know. You all make so much noise I could hear you a mile away."

"All clear?" asked Clyde.

"Well, would we be sittin' here flappin' our jaws if it weren't? I rid a wide loop all around this hole and didn't see nary a-thing to point my ears at. So let's go on in. You all spread out and keep them horses on tight rein."

They emerged from the brush-choked slope well-spaced, holding their mounts to the walk, their

eyes alert, hands on their guns. Like buzzards closing in on a fresh carcass, they converged on the
cabin.

Ogham was dashing handfuls of water up under
his arms when horse-whicker spun him around.
Recognizing the riders breaking cover, he breathed
a sigh of relief. When he saw the bulging gunnysacks, one tied to Black Jack's saddle and the other
on Clyde's, greed glimmered in his piggish eyes.

"Howdy, boys!" he called as he walked to meet
them. "Looks like you had some luck."

"Yeah," said Black Jack. "We rustled some of
them new government greenbacks."

"Jack!"

Mattie raced across the hardpack. Black Jack
swept her up in one brawny arm and gave her a hard
kiss. When he let go she hung on, her arms around
his neck. Chuckling, he pried her loose and lowered
her to the ground.

"Pop," he said, "we come for fresh mounts."

"I figured. Knew you didn't come calling for tea
and crumpets. But truth is I ain't got none. Just
come back from trailing a passel of cows up to Colorado, and I ain't had the time or the inclination to
rustle up a batch of nags."

"Well ain't that a kick in the pants?" The kind
of man who took every misfortune in stride, Black
Jack barked a laugh. Then he gave Mattie, the
cabin, and the surrounding heights a long, slow
once-over. His gaze came to rest on the old rewrite
man. "Seen any sign of John Law hereabouts?"

Ogham snickered. "Taint none, 'less you brought 'em."

"They hounded us to the Sunset Rim, but I reckon we lost 'em last night. Ask me, they're back in Hanksville by now, nursin' their saddle blisters."

"Where's the half-breed?"

"Swope's place. His horse come up lame. The breed didn't want to give that racer up. Decided to stay with Swope for a spell."

Ogham nodded. He didn't trust copperbellies or greasers, and a man with both kinds of blood in him was twice as untrustworthy, in his studied opinion.

"Reckon you'll find some of O'Reilly's stock over by Crow Seep. He wouldn't much mind were you to swap with him."

Black Jack glanced at the men who rode with him. He did not fail to notice the way Shad Mowry was watching Mattie Ogham.

"Clyde," he said, "you take Shad and jingle us some of that Irishman's stock. I think I'll wait for you here. The Lukans will stick with me. I got me a few saddle blisters of my own to nurse." He grinned at Mattie.

Clyde nodded. He knew exactly why his brother had a notion to dally at the Ogham place. He also knew why Black Jack was sending Mowry with him.

As he rode away, the taciturn Mowry in tow, Clyde decided that one day soon blood was going to spill on account of that yellow-haired girl.

CHAPTER 7

WHEN HE CAME TO, SLATER WAS SURPRISED to be alive.

Spitting dirt, he rolled over and sat up, wincing at the white-hot agony exploding in his skull. He gingerly felt the back of his head. Dried blood matted his hair.

The late afternoon shadows of the cottonwoods reached for him across the hardpack. Then he realized something besides cottonwoods was casting shadow, and he looked up to see two bodies hanging from one of the trees. One was Swope. Next to him was the half-breed outlaw. Why had Whitmore and the others bothered hanging a dead man? Slater had no idea. He'd given up trying to figure people out a long time ago.

The sheriff's body lay nearby. Slater thought it was mighty confederate of Whitmore and the Hanksville posse to take their leave without bothering to plant the lawman. Whitmore, no doubt, had believed it to be a waste of time.

Slater's hand dropped to his holster. The Schofield was still there. As he made this welcome discovery, the canelo came out of the barn, whickering over a mouthful of hay, and walking primly to avoid the dragging reins. Slater smiled grimly. Whitmore had made one mistake by leaving him alive, then made another by not confiscating his horse and weapons.

Getting slowly to his feet, he waited until the earth ceased to move before making for the well. Cranking up the bucket, he poured its contents over his head. Then he went into the house, hunted up a shovel, and went to work digging graves beneath the hanging tree.

He didn't mind taking the time to put the dead men under. Wherever Black Jack Bohannon went, Slater was confident he could find him. He didn't worry about the posse beating him to it. Like as not, the Hanksville men would wind up lost and going around in circles. Getting lost in the Devil's Kitchen was not difficult. Slater concluded that nothing would be gained by rattling the canelo's hocks trying to make a few miles before nightfall. Anyway, the horse had gorged itself on Swope's fodder. Run hard, it would founder for sure.

Only shreds of daylight lingered in the sky by

the time he had finished digging three shallow graves. Using his clasp knife, he sawed at the ropes where they were tied off to the tree trunk. Swope fell directly into his grave. The breed missed by half. Slater rolled him in the rest of the way. He dragged Hanksville's ex-sheriff across the yard and deposited him into the third hole. He didn't bother saying any words over the dead. He didn't know any of those kinds of words.

Shoveling dirt on the breed's face, Slater wondered if he was burying a man with a price on his head. He knew by heart the descriptions of half a hundred wanted men. The breed was unknown to him, and he was not inclined to haul the body all over creation and the Devil's Kitchen on the off chance he could turn it in for a reward.

He felt a little sorry for Swope. Sometimes life didn't give a man a fair chance. From personal experience, Slater could testify to that. When his uncle had assaulted Slater's cousin that dark Montana night years ago, Slater had seen no alternative but to intervene. His action had cost him dearly, changed his life forever, but he wasn't one to cry over spilt milk. His time with the Apaches had taught him that much. What happened, happened, good or bad—and most of it was bad. In all things, a dark streak of adopted Indian fatalism affected Slater's outlook.

Tamping down the mounded earth with the flat of the shovel, Slater considered gathering enough rocks to pile over the graves. If he didn't, varmints were likely to dig the corpses up. He decided, though, not to trouble himself. Scavengers or worms, what did it matter? Nature took Her course, and no man could stop Her. It was enough that he had given the three dead men a proper burial. In Slater's mind, that was every man's last right.

His head throbbing with pain made worse by recent exertion, he slumped to the ground near the graves and leaned back against a cottonwood, closing his eyes to dancing pinpricks of white light. He listened to the wind whispering in the trees, the song of a meadowlark, and felt the earth cool beneath him as night came stalking.

He reflected on the irony of his situation. His only reason for accepting the sheriff's invitation to join the Hanksville posse was to protect its members, well-meaning amateurs, from Bohannon and from themselves. It seemed they weren't so well-meaning, after all; certainly not worth his misplaced concern for their welfare. He should have known better. Was there really much difference between the lawless and the law-abiding? Slater didn't think so. Another lesson learned.

Later, he led the canelo away from the Swope place, and set up a cold camp in a bunch of cedar a few hundred yards away. Apparently Swope had lived alone. The house was empty, and there for the using, but Slater preferred the stars over his head to a roof.

Dawn caught him on the day-old trail of the Bohannon gang. A few miles from the Swope place, he found where the Hanksville posse had lost the trail on slickrock. Slater wasn't at all surprised.

As a precaution, Bohannon had used the rocky terrain to full advantage, doubling back and leaving the area in an entirely different direction from the one he had been keeping to before. Slater guessed the outlaws had used rawhide "boots" on the hooves of their horses. It was an old Indian trick Slater had employed a time or two himself.

Two sets of tracks left the slickrock area, one heading northeast, the other northwest. The former was the posse, the latter Bohannon's bunch. Slater was certain of this. Yesterday he had tracked the Bohannon gang. Now he recognized their sign by several distinctive shoe markings.

He followed the sign through a line of sand hills and up a game trail onto a rock-strewn tableland. Half an hour later he was letting the canelo pick its way down a shale slope into a deep and twisting canyon. This he negotiated in a northerly direction and came eventually to a narrow side canyon choked with brush.

Into this he ventured until the smell of woodsmoke alerted him. Dismounting, he led the canelo up a steep draw. Tethering the horse to a gnarled greasewood, he pulled his Spencer 56/50 from the saddle and proceeded on foot. He climbed to a rock outcropping that jutted from the canyon wall. From this vantage point he could look down into a hidden basin and see the cabin.

The cabin had been built with upright cedar

posts, in the manner of a stockade. As the trees in the Devil's Kitchen grew short and twisted, it was much simpler to construct walls in this manner, rather than laying them flat and trying to splice them together. Mud had been used to caulk the spaces between the posts. The roof was covered with a thick layer of red gypsum clay. Slater assumed that beneath the clay was a second layer of cedar bark laid out on more cedar posts.

From his position Slater could see the front porch, the door, and a small side window draped with burlap curtains. A wisp of smoke curled lazily out of a stone chimney.

Across a stretch of hardpack from the front of the cabin was a wooden sluice angling down a brushy slope, depositing a steady trickle of water into a trough. Slater took this to mean that a spring existed on the limestone ledge above the sluice. Beyond the cabin was a corral, fenced on three sides, the fourth being a sheer rock face.

Slater counted three horses in the corral. He took thirty minutes to scan the slopes all around. No sign of a lookout. What had happened to the other two horses he had tracked, and the riders who went with them? He had to find out.

He took his time—two hours to work his way completely around the basin, keeping to the high ground as much as possible. He watched for a lookout and searched for sign, moving like an Apache, silent and unseen.

Eventually he found the tracks of the two missing horses, dipping down into a wash and then beneath a natural arch and through a narrow cut. So the side canyon wasn't a box after all. There was a back way out. A perfect outlaw hideout, hard to find, easy to get out of.

Returning to the rock outcrop, Slater found a speck of shade and settled down to wait. No one, as far as he knew, had emerged from the cabin in the past three hours. He had no idea how many people were in there. Probably just three, all members of the Bohannon gang. But which ones? Was Black Jack down there? Or was he one of the pair which had moved on? Time would tell.

Slater's patience knew no bounds. He would wait until they came out, and kill them at long range. If he could avoid it, he wouldn't give them a chance. Fair play was for fools.

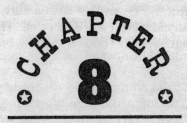

CHAPTER 8

WHITMORE WAS A MAN WHO KNEW HIS LIMITA-
tions. He believed himself to be an astute business-
man, and to be successful in business you had to
know your own strengths and weaknesses, as well
as the strengths and weaknesses of others.

For instance, he knew perfectly well that he did
not possess the requisite experience to follow outlaw sign across rough country. This was the reason
he prevailed upon the T Anchor range rider, the
young cowboy named Bryner, to take the point and
keep the Hanksville posse on the trail of the Bohannon gang.

When Bryner failed him, Whitmore lost his temper. He railed and ranted, and the more he did, the
darker the cowboy's features became. Bryner stood

there tightlipped, fists clenched, until Whitmore had spent his wrath. Then he wiped Whitmore's spit off his face and stepped up into his saddle. He swept the rest of the posse with a grim gaze.

"I reckon I'll be headed back," he said, very quietly.

"Wait," said Whitmore, becoming calm and reasonable so suddenly that the others really started to worry. "Wait. Don't go. You can't go. We've got to get Bohannon. We're a posse. We have a solemn duty to perform."

"Duty?" asked Ricker. "That what it was when we lynched Swope?"

Mutiny was in the air. Whitmore felt it, and grasped at straws.

"Stoddard, the sheriff put you in charge. You can order the others to stay on. We don't turn back unless you say. Are you going to let Bohannon get away? My God, man! Three good men are dead, including Elledge. The sheriff was your friend."

Stoddard thought it peculiar that Whitmore was suddenly shifting the burden of command to his shoulders. Since leaving the Swope place, Whitmore had been carrying on like he was in charge.

"We got the man what done for Elledge," said Stoddard. "Or I should say Slater did."

Mention of the bounty hunter's name caused all the men but Whitmore and McVey to exchange anxious looks.

"We should have killed Slater when we had the chance," said McVey.

Stoddard, Bryner and Ricker looked back at the young gunhawk. They had all but forgotten he was present. Bringing up the rear of the posse, McVey had not uttered a word all day.

"You could've said he took a bullet in the shoot-out," said McVey. "You could've shot Swope, instead of stringing him up, and said the same."

Bryner squinted at the midday sun. There wasn't a cloud in sight. The sun was a blazing inferno, laying its heavy hand upon the Devil's Kitchen. The land was a furnace. Heat hammered down from the sky, came simmering out of the rocky red ground, and hung in the breathless air, a visible haze. He was beginning to wonder if he had died and gone to hell.

"I reckon I'll be headed back," he said again, shifting uncomfortably in his sweat-darkened saddle. But, as before, he did not put spurs to horse.

Truth was, he didn't know what to do. No one else did, either. All had reached the same conclusion: they were in big trouble. They had done wrong. The only way out was to stick together, but Bryner didn't much care for their company, and expected they felt the same.

Whitmore read them, and read them right. "If we get Bohannon," he said softly, "we'll all be heroes."

Stoddard nodded. "It's the only way I can see to set things aright."

Whitmore tried to restrain a smile that tugged at the corners of his mouth. He had them. Wiping sweat off his forehead with a sleeve, he climbed stiffly aboard his horse.

"We'll backtrack 'til we find their trail," he said.

It was the only course to take, and they took it, but by late afternoon it became apparent to everyone that they had somehow managed to lose even their own trail.

As the day finally drew to a close, they were crossing a rocky bench above a cedar-thick valley, riding single-file and slumped in their saddles, tired and despondent. The craggy heights above were bright orange in the sunset. Below, the blue shadows of dusk were gathering in the valley.

It was Bryner who saw the campfire first. Stoddard, Ricker and Whitmore, townfolk all, were by now so wrapped up in the agony which all this unaccustomed riding had bestowed upon them that they were scarcely paying any attention whatsoever to the countryside.

Encouraged and at the same time apprehensive, the Hanksville posse hurried down off the bench and into the cover of the lowland cedar. Bryner, swallowing his fear, volunteered to scout ahead. He was gone a long time. Night closed in around the others, and nerves wore thin. They were as jumpy as turpentined cats when the T Anchor hand returned, and Ricker almost shot him.

"I got close enough to see five horses on a stake rope," said Bryner.

"Is it Bohannon and his gang?" hissed Whitmore, impatient.

"The men were around the fire, on the other side of the horses from me, and down in some kind of hollow. There's a creek down yonder. I couldn't get around the horses without stepping out into the open. I tried to listen, but they weren't talkin' much. I did hear someone say something about a bank, and someone else said something about a posse, but I couldn't make it out. They're bein' mighty quiet."

"It must be Bohannon," said Stoddard. "Five men. Who else could it be?"

"Let's go get 'em," said Whitmore. He didn't want to give the others time to think about what they were getting themselves into. "We'll leave our horses out a ways and slip in on foot."

"I dunno," muttered Bryner dubiously. "If things go sour I'd just as soon be with my horse."

"We'll walk the horses in as close as we can," said McVey, "then mount up and ride right through 'em, shooting anything that moves." The others stared at him. He added, "It's the way the Texas Rangers do it. You've got the advantages of speed and surprise. It's hard to hit a mounted man when he's moving fast."

"Fine," said Whitmore. "Gallop and gunshot. We'll give Bohannon a taste of his own medicine."

He led the way through the woods, taking the path of least resistance around thick clumps of scrub cedar. The ground was dust and shale. The iron-shod hooves of their horses clacked and clattered, and the noise was painfully loud in Whitmore's ears. How could the outlaws fail to hear their approach?

It was plenty dark now. Too early for the moon, but even Whitmore could stay on course in this instance. The little valley was narrow, sloping down to the creek, and all he had to do was keep the brawling run and the downhill slant on his right side.

Getting closer, they saw the firelight against the trees, though the fire itself was hidden from view in the hollow. Whitmore mounted, and the rest followed suit, drawing their guns.

Whitmore led them on. He figured it was safer to be the first man through the enemy camp, rather than the last. The desperadoes would be quick to recover from their surprise. His throat was parchment dry, his heart racing. He prayed for the first time in years. Not for his own survival, but for the privilege of being the one to kill Black Jack Bohannon.

Holding his horse to a walk, he almost blundered into the picketed mounts Bryner had reported. One of the horses on the stake rope whickered loudly. A voice was raised in the camp beyond. Whitmore kicked his horse into a high lope.

The Hanksville posse surged forward. Yellow spurts of flame filled the hollow. Whitmore caught a glimpse of the men in camp scattering like quail as his horse leaped over the fire. Gun thunder deafened him as he fired point-blank into the back of the man who was reaching for a rifle slanted across a saddle. He didn't even see the man fall. The next thing he knew, his horse had charged straight into a cedar thicket, almost sweeping him off the saddle. Whitmore clawed his way out of the tangle, cursing vehemently, and emerged to find the rest of the posse near at hand, trying to reload and at the same time get their prancing, blowing mounts under control. They were well out of the camp now.

"Anybody hit?" asked Stoddard, breathless.

They checked themselves, then each other, and no one seemed to be hurt.

"I got one," announced Whitmore.

"Let's go through 'em again!" yelled McVey, his voice high-pitched, and in the next instant he was gut-hooking his horse back into the hollow.

"Wait a minute!" called Bryner. "You knock down a hornet's nest, you don't go back to pick it up."

No one was listening, but they should have. As they charged down into the hollow again, Stoddard cutting loose with a Rebel yell, they found no one to shoot at. One man lay facedown—the one Whitmore had backshot. The rest had drifted into the dark woods, making for their horses, and as the posse reappeared in the clearing, a ragged volley greeted them. Whitmore heard the angry scream of hot lead and saw Ricker somersault over the haunches of his horse.

It occurred to Whitmore that they had made a mistake by not scattering the outlaws' horses. Then he stopped thinking, for his horse was hit and going down, nosediving into the dirt, and he was hurled twenty feet.

Stunned, he lay there, flat on his back, and dimly heard a smattering of gunfire, then felt the vibration of horses on the run. The gunfire abruptly ceased, and he heard next the unmistakable sound of someone being violently sick. He sat up, squeezing his eyes tightly shut as the world spun madly. When he opened them, he saw the trembling legs of a hard-run horse, and looked up at McVey. Relieved, he swallowed the lump in his throat.

"They're long gone," said McVey, and his voice echoed strangely in Whitmore's head, as though they were both at the bottom of a deep well. "We'll never catch 'em in the dark."

Whitmore grabbed hold of McVey's offside saddle fender and hauled himself upright. He took a slow look around the clearing. His horse was dead. Ricker lay spread-eagle yonder, and somehow Whitmore knew the burly blacksmith was as dead as the horse. Stoddard was leaning precariously out of his saddle, dry-heaving. Soogans and saddles were scattered everywhere. The outlaws had lit a shuck bareback. The trampled fire was nothing more than a scatter of orange embers billowing pale smoke.

Bryner was checking the body of the man Whitmore had killed.

"Recognize him?" asked Whitmore.

"Matter of fact, I do," murmured the T Anchor cowboy, his voice hollow. He straightened and looked strangely at Whitmore, his face bone-white in the night gloom. "It's Will Ashley, the Moab sheriff."

"Oh my God!" moaned Stoddard.

Whitmore stumbled forward on uncertain legs, looked for himself. Bryner had rolled the dead man over, and though he didn't recognize him, Whitmore knew a lawman's badge when he saw one.

"How could this happen?" groaned Stoddard.

Whitmore understood it all, then, with perfect clarity. How it had happened, and what they had to do about it. Sheriff Elledge had wired news of the bank robbery to Moab, and Ashley here had led a posse into the Devil's Kitchen from the east.

"Damn you, Elledge," he muttered.

"What did you say?" asked Bryner.

"He should've told us," said Whitmore, talking to himself. "No. I should have known."

"You killed the Moab sheriff," said Bryner.

"Thanks for telling me."

"We're all gonna hang," said Stoddard.

"No we won't," said Whitmore, surprised at how calmly and clearly he was thinking. "The Bohannon gang did this. Those Moab men won't know any different. All they know is a bunch of hombres came out of the dark and started shooting. They were too busy trying to save their hides to get a good look. We'll blame it on Bohannon."

He gave each of them a long hard look in turn, taking the measure of each man. He decided he could rely on McVey to do whatever was necessary in the desperate days ahead. He wasn't so sure of Stoddard and Bryner.

They couldn't afford to make any more mistakes, so Whitmore took an extra moment to think it through. Ricker's body would have to disappear. His saddle, too. He would put his own saddle on Ricker's horse. *His* horse presented a problem—evidence they could not readily dispose of. Chances were good the Moab posse wouldn't return. Like as not, they wouldn't stop running 'til they reached home ground. But if they did, and found the horse, could they trace it back to him? Whitmore doubted it. If they did, he would think of something. He would have to. He sure as hell wasn't going to hang.

He bent over and plucked the badge from Ashley's shirt front.

"What are you doing?" asked Bryner.

"When we take Bohannon's body back, they'll find this badge on him. That will tie him into this tighter than a squaw knot."

"One problem," said McVey. "The bounty hunter. He's probably on Bohannon's trail right now. What if he takes Bohannon's body back? He'll know Bohannon wasn't anywhere near here."

Whitmore nodded.

"I know. I've thought about that. We've just got to make sure Slater doesn't leave these mountains alive."

CHAPTER 9

THE SCORPION CRAWLED ONTO SLATER'S LEG and paused there, feeling the slow and measured pulse of the man through the heavy twill of his pants. Slater watched the deadly creature without a trace of apprehension on his sun-dark face. He could sweep the scorpion away with one quick stroke of his arm, but he didn't bother.

Almost everything that walked, flew, crawled, or grew in this country could do harm. Slater had learned long ago to live with the land rather than against it. He knew the scorpion would not use the hollow, poison-filled stinger at the tip of its armored tail unless he made a hostile or frightened move. His pulse remained steady, and the scorpion lost interest and crawled away, off one leg and across the other.

Slater's ice-blue gaze swept the rimrock. In moments the morning sun would appear, immediately filling the canyon with breathless heat. All night he had waited in the outcropping of rocks on the slope above the cabin. He wasn't watching the place, relying instead on his acute hearing. Even at this distance he was confident he would hear anyone stirring down below in the hidden basin. Late into the night he had dimly heard voices raised from within the cabin, and he now believed there was a woman with the three longriders.

Only once since yesterday had Slater left the rocks, returning to the hillside draw to give the canelo some water, and himself a little less. He had gathered a few clumps of mesquite grass and tanglehead to feed the horse, as the canelo had not touched the greasewood to which it was tethered. Also known in these parts as the creosote, the greasewood burned with a bright, quick flame, and some oldtimers swore by its resin as a treatment for rheumatism. The greasewood was unpalatable to animals, which was why Slater had tied the canelo to it in the first place. Nothing better than a fool horse yanking the leaves off brittle branches if you wanted to give your presence away to the enemy.

Now the faint aroma of woodsmoke reached him, and Slater almost smiled. Good. They were alive and kicking in the cabin. Sooner or later someone would come out for fresh water, or to relieve himself, or to check on the horses in the corral.

Slater found himself wishing for a bow and arrow. That way, he could kill silently at long distance. He was a better than fair hand with the bow, thanks to Apache tutoring. He knew how to make one out of mulberry wood, strengthened with deer horn, and he could fashion arrows from carrizo reed, with hawk-feather fletching. But today he would have to make do with the Spencer 56/50 lying across his legs.

The sun crawled above the peaks, striking him with a hammer of heat, and Slater leaped to his feet. It wasn't the heat that moved him, but the faint sound of an angel singing.

He didn't hear it any longer. Wait. There it was again. Very faint, reaching him in snatches, carried on the fickle wind or off the stony flanks of the canyon.

Sister Rachel.

It couldn't be. But it was. Sister Rachel, she of the angel's voice, making her way up the canyon. Surely not in that rickety spring wagon. No way a wagon could get into this side canyon.

He wondered if the Right Reverend Joshua Hazen was with her, and if they had any idea what kind of trouble they were blundering into. And he wondered if he should try to warn them, because if they kept coming up-canyon they were going to meet some of those lost souls they were looking to save. Slater figured the reverend and Sister Rachel—especially Sister Rachel—were going to be the ones in dire need of salvation.

The last time he'd tried being helpful was agreeing to join the Hanksville posse. What had he gotten in return? A near-broken skull. It was past time he learned to let folks make their own mistakes.

Problem was, out here you didn't always live far enough past the first mistake to profit from the experience.

The singing grew steadily louder. "Onward Christian Soldiers." The song brought a flood of unpleasant memories. His mother had been very religious—when he'd mentioned to Reverend Hazen that his folks had been God-fearing, he hadn't been making it up. He had a vague and disturbing recollection of his mother praying, the instant before a Sioux lance went clean through her body.

A shout dragged him back to the present, and he slipped between two boulders and glanced down into the basin. A man stood in front of the cabin, and another quickly emerged to join him. Slater recognized them. The Lukan brothers. Not a dime's worth of difference between them. Lanky, yellow-haired, dressed like sodbusters, and not a single redeeming virtue to their name.

Slater brought the Spencer to bear on them. Then he lowered the carbine. Black Jack Bohannon was still inside the cabin. If he dropped the Lukans now he'd play hell getting Black Jack out without burning the place down, and he still didn't know about the woman he had heard last night. One thing he did know: he wouldn't be responsible for her death if there was any possible way around it.

"Come on, Black Jack," he whispered. "Stick your ugly face out of there for just a minute."

The outlaws had heard the singing. They were as bewildered as Slater and the posse had been two mornings ago at the Sunset Rim *hueco.*

One of the Lukans went back inside. Slater couldn't tell which; the "paper" on the brothers gave one general description for both. He came back out with gunbelts and rifles, which he shared with his twin. One headed into the brush on the ridge beyond the water trough. The other sought cover behind a pile of rocks directly below Slater's vantage point. Slater shook his head, disgusted. They were setting up an ambush, which meant Bohannon wasn't coming out of the cabin until the trap had been sprung.

Slater turned his attention down-canyon. A moment later the angel and the Bible-thumper hove into view. They were riding the mules bareback, single file, with the reverend in the lead, sticking to a narrow trail that snaked through the rocks and the catclaw and the occasional scrub cedar. Slater wasn't worried about them spotting him or his horse. And they weren't going to see the cabin, either, until it was too late—until the trail curled around a tongue of shale and into the basin. That they would know woodsmoke when they smelled it was, he supposed, too much to hope for.

It occurred to him that this could turn out to

be a blessing in disguise. When Sister Rachel and the reverend reached the cabin, Black Jack would be quick to realize they posed no threat. There was a good chance he would come out into the open, off guard and a prime target for Slater, waiting up in the rocks like a rattlesnake coiled around a prairie dog hole.

So he remained in the outcropping, and let the scene unfold.

Hazen and the sister rode into the basin and right up to the cabin, and when the reverend called out to ask if anyone was home the Lukans broke cover and converged from opposite directions. Rachel and the reverend slid off the mules, and only then did Bohannon come out of the cabin.

Slater had a bead drawn on Black Jack's barrel chest, and his finger squeezing the trigger, when the young woman emerged and happened to stand directly in Slater's line of fire, at Bohannon's side. Some said Black Jack had a charmed life, and Slater was beginning to believe it.

The early morning sun was slanting up under the poles of the porch roof, and Slater could see Black Jack's ear-to-ear grin.

"Better search 'em, boys," he said. "You cain't be too careful these days."

The Lukans closed in on Hazen. While one held a gun to the reverend's head, the other did the frisking. Hazen held his hands high, a Bible clutched in one of them.

When it came time to search Sister Rachel, a

quarrel broke out between the Lukans. Black Jack barked a sharp reprimand. One of the brothers put his rifle on the ground, got behind Sister Rachel and grabbed her around the waist, holding her tight against him. The other started his frisk by groping her breasts. Her high-collared dress of stiff brown serge was in his way, so he began to tug and tear at it. Hazen lurched forward with a high-pitched protest. The Lukan doing the damage to Sister Rachel's garment paused long enough to backhand the reverend into the dirt. Hazen sprawled, losing his spectacles.

Sister Rachel remained as stoic as a martyr. Even with one Lukan squeezing the breath out of her and the other roughly fondling her now uncovered breasts, she did not scream or fight back.

Slater saw the yellow-haired girl in front of the cabin whirl to confront Bohannon. She said something in a fierce whisper, and Slater couldn't make it out, but clearly she did not much care for what the Lukans were up to. Black Jack ignored her, grinning as he watched the brothers having their fun.

Recovering his spectacles, Reverend Hazen stood up and opened his Bible. This, thought Slater, was one hell of a time to start sermonizing.

But it was a pocket pistol, not gospel, that Joshua Hazen took from the Good Book.

He put the gun to the head of the Lukan doing the mauling and fired at point-blank range. Lukan crumpled. The other Lukan let go of Sister Rachel faster than he would a hot skillet. Hazen fired again, and the second Lukan went down, but he wasn't done for, and grabbed for his sidegun. Sister Rachel spun, kicked it out of his grasp, groped under her skirt, and came out with a revolver, with which she put an end to the career of the last Lukan brother.

Black Jack was quick to react. He grabbed the yellow-haired girl and pulled her roughly in front of him, drew his pistol and fired—all in one fast, fluid motion.

Hazen spun and fell to his knees. Rachel fired, aiming high and parting Bohannon's hair. Black Jack ducked hastily into the cabin, dragging the yellow-haired girl with him. Rachel threw a quick look at Hazen. He was still kneeling in the pale dust, his head bowed, looking for all the world like a man deep in prayer. The spectacles, hanging askew from one ear, fell to the ground. Slater saw sunlight flash off the wire rims, and then Hazen was falling forward, crushing the see-betters under his dead weight.

Bohannon came through the rear wall of the cabin. There wasn't a door—he simply bulled through the upright cedar poles, shattering the dry, dead wood. Rachel heard the racket and angled for the corral at a run. *Smart,* thought Slater. Black Jack headed for the corral, but Rachel cut him off with a couple of shots, and Bohannon wasted no time changing direction, charging up the steep slope behind the cabin.

The yellow-haired girl bolted out of the cabin by

way of the front door, screaming hoarsely, and started after the outlaw leader. Slater didn't know what her problem was, and he didn't care. He hadn't once had a clear shot at Bohannon, and he wasn't one to waste ammunition on maybes, but now he saw his chance.

He fired. Bohannon fell, sliding ten feet on his face in an avalanche of rock rubble. Levering another round into the breech, Slater stepped clear of the rocks and put stock to shoulder again. He didn't think Bohannon was quite dead, and he was right, because Black Jack rolled over on his side, and his pistol spit flame. The bullet slapped stone behind Slater, very near the spot from which he had fired the first shot.

Slater fired again. The yellow-haired girl's screaming went up a notch. She reached Bohannon and threw her body across his. Slater grimaced. In his studied opinion, one more bullet in Black Jack was called for, but the girl prevented him from making the insurance shot.

He closed in quickly, angling down the sharp slope, nimbly keeping his balance in spite of the treacherous shale under foot. He saw Rachel running toward Black Jack. They arrived simultaneously. Slater bent down and twisted the revolver out of Bohannon's weak grasp. The yellow-haired girl looked hatefully at Slater, her eyes wet with tears.

"You bastard!" she screamed. "You killed him!"

"I didn't come all this way to shake hands," said Slater.

Bohannon wasn't quite gone under. His eyes fluttered open. Drooling blood, he grinned up at Slater. Slater noted that he had hit Black Jack twice in the chest. *This*, he mused, *was one tough customer.*

"You done put the hurt on me, stranger," rasped Bohannon.

"Nothin' personal."

Black Jack barked a pain-wracked laugh. "Nothin' personal. That's rich. Bounty hunter?"

"Right."

Bohannon turned his head to look at Rachel. She was aiming her pistol at him, a double-action, .32 caliber Savage. *The perfect hideout gun,* thought Slater. She'd lost her bonnet, and her chestnut hair, come undone, caught fire in the sun. Lukan had seriously damaged the serge dress, exposing full, firm breasts white as alabaster, but she didn't seem at all concerned with modesty or decorum at the moment.

Gazing at her breasts, Bohannon leered. "Hope the angels look half as good where I'm going," he said.

"They don't have angels where you're going," she replied.

Black Jack coughed, convulsed, and heaved up a lot of blood, spraying the yellow-haired girl with it. "Ain't life a bitch?" he wheezed, strangling, and then his body went limp. He died still grinning.

Slater looked at Rachel. "Know any good hymns?"

Her eyes were hard and emerald-green. "I've sung my last hymn, thank God."

"You have a good singing voice."

"And you're a very good shot." Suddenly the .32 Savage was aimed rock-steady at his chest. "So please drop your weapons."

The yellow-haired girl rose and backed away from Bohannon's body. She paid no attention to Slater or Rachel, just stared at the corpse and wiped a stray tear from her cheek.

"Damn," she said petulantly. "Now I'll never get those purty dresses he promised."

CHAPTER 10

"DROP THE GUNS," SAID RACHEL AGAIN, MORE sharply than before. "I don't want to kill you unless I have to. Ammunition costs money, and your scalp isn't worth a plugged nickel. You see, I try not to kill anybody who isn't papered."

"A woman after my own heart," said Slater. At least she didn't know about the dead-or-alive reward Montana was offering for him.

"I'm not going to tell you again . . . ."

Moving slowly, Slater laid the Spencer and Bohannon's revolver on the ground.

"Gunbelt," said Rachel.

Slater unbuckled his gunbelt and dropped it beside the other weapons.

"I have the feeling we've met before," he said.

"A few years ago—Rio Bravo. You killed the *pistolero*, Madrid, before I could get to him."

Slater nodded. Now he remembered.

"Rachel Myers. How could I forget such a pretty face?"

"You carry any hideouts?"

"That's your specialty."

"Slater, I plan to take Black Jack Bohannon in for the reward. Do you plan to try and stop me?"

"No."

She smiled. "You're lying. Bohannon's worth $2,000."

"Two thousand," murmured the yellow-haired girl, staring at Black Jack's corpse.

Rachel glanced at her. "Just who are you, anyway?"

"Mattie. Mattie Ogham. I live here."

"Alone?"

"Not alone," said Slater. " 'Cause there's a man just come out of the cabin behind you."

"That's an old trick, Slater."

Slater shrugged. "Suit yourself."

Rachel heard the clatter of a gate pole dropping, followed by the nervous whicker of a horse. She backed away a few steps and threw a quick look in the direction of the corral. The three horses were acting up, and then she saw a man in the swirling dust. The man jumped onto the bare back of one of the horses and slapped, kicked, and hoorawed the mount out through the open gate.

"Damn," said Rachel, and brought the Savage to bear on the rider.

"No!" screamed Mattie, and hurled herself bodily into Rachel. Both women tumbled down the slope. Slater picked up the Spencer and drew a bead on the rider. Like Rachel, his first instinct was to drop the man trying to get away; a purely predatory reflex, but he thought better of it. He didn't know who the man was or why he was running. Or, most important, if he was worth killing.

So he held his fire and strolled down the shale slope, stepping on the Savage which Rachel had lost in her head-over-heels descent, and which she was now trying to recover in a hurry. On hands and knees, she glowered up at him.

"Damn it!" she breathed. "Damn it, damn it, damn it!"

"Not very ladylike."

"Go to hell."

The man on horseback was out of the basin by now. Mattie lay, semi-conscious, a few feet beyond Rachel.

"I should have remembered you," remarked Slater. "But your hair was black then."

"Madrid preferred the senoritas."

"I reckon he would have also preferred dying in bed."

Rachel stood and brushed herself off. *An odd gesture*, thought Slater, considering the wrecked condition of her dress. She had scraped elbow and cheek in the fall.

"Speaking of which," she said, a corner of her mouth curling in a wanton half-smile, "maybe we can strike a deal."

"Sure. You killed the Lukans, you can collect on 'em. I killed Bohannon, so I'll take him in."

"I went to a lot of trouble to get Black Jack Bohannon!" she protested. "It isn't fair! I would have had him if you hadn't butted in. I got manhandled. I lost my partner. I had to sing stupid hymns until I was blue in the face. . ."

"Sorry, sister."

"I went through a lot to get Black Jack Bohannon, and I would have done it, too, except for you. It's not fair."

"I reckon the worst of it was having to act like a proper young Christian lady. And if you're trying to tell me you're bothered by what the Lukans did to you, I'm not buying it."

She just stood there and stared at him for a full half-minute. Finally she seemed to give in to the inevitable, and stuck out her hand.

"You're right. You should collect on Bohannon. I'll just have to settle for the $500 apiece the Lukan brothers will bring. Let's call a truce, Slater. What do you say?"

Slater didn't say anything, and he didn't shake her hand. He climbed back up to Bohannon's body, recovered his gunbelt, and buckled it back on. Then he snugged Rachel's .32 Savage under the belt in back, and Black Jack's revolver in front.

He remembered Rachel Myers, all right, and

that was why he couldn't trust a word she said. She was something of a legend, and not just because she was the only female bounty hunter anyone knew about. Truth was, woman or no, she was damned good at what she did. Miss Bounty, they called her. She had tracked down and dealt with some of the roughest papered men on the frontier. Precisely because she *was* a woman she often got closer to an outlaw than any of her male counterparts could even hope to.

Part and parcel of the legend of Rachel Myers was that she always slept with a man before killing him. Slater couldn't know if that was true in every case, but apparently she *had* been trying to lure the Rio Bravo gunfighter, Johnny Madrid, into a trap by using her obvious charms. Only Slater had gunned Madrid down before Miss Bounty could do her black widow spider routine.

Slater started back down the slope. Mattie was sitting up now, her head hanging low, and she didn't look up as he passed her. Rachel was crossing the hardpack in front of the cabin, making for the body of the late Joshua Hazen. Slater lengthened his stride, and arrived as she was bending over to pick up the pocket pistol which Hazen had used to kill one of the Lukans. It was a Remington derringer, a .41 caliber rimfire, with over-and-under barrels and a stud trigger. Hazen had fired both barrels, so Slater breathed easier. Rachel smiled wryly.

"Don't you trust me?" she asked, mocking him.

Slater picked up the big leather-bound Bible

and held it out, the spine lying across his palm. The Bible fell open, and he saw the derringer-shaped cavity cut into the pages.

Rachel obediently put the Remington in the Bible, shaking her head. "This is no way for some-one to treat his new partner."

"We're not partners."

"Slater . . ."

"I work alone."

"I usually do, too." She glanced at Hazen's body. "Why him?"

She shrugged. "Because he was an unprinci-pled, cold-blooded killer, that's why. He was good at what he did."

"Not good enough. He didn't know his Scripture very well, and he wasn't much of a hand at driving a rig."

"You don't cut slack for anybody, do you? He was an Easterner; hailed from New York City. He said he was a policeman. Apparently a corrupt one, on the payroll of an organization called Tammany Hall. He killed people. When things got too hot for him he came West. I thought I might need a little help with the Bohannon gang."

She searched Slater's face a moment, looking very serious.

"Listen, Slater. We can help each other. We're a hundred miles from the nearest town, in the heart of outlaw country. When Bohannon's brother Clyde finds out about this he'll be after us both with blood in his eye. One word, and he'll have twenty or thirty hardcases riding with him. Be sensible."

"All right. We'll ride together until we get to Hanksville. Or until you try something and I have to shoot you."

His easy acquiescence made her suspicious. "You mean it?"

Slater nodded in the direction of the corral. "Why don't you check out the cabin while I saddle those two horses? Maybe you'll find something to wear." He smiled, looking her over. "You could get a bad case of sunburn."

"Can I have my gun back?"

"Later."

"What about Hazen?"

"What about him?"

"Should we bury him?"

"I reckon."

Rachel nodded, and headed for the cabin. Slater watched her go. He figured there was a good chance she'd find a weapon in there. He hadn't changed his mind about trusting her. It just made more sense to keep her in sight. Sooner or later she would try something, and now was as good a time as any to give her the opportunity.

Mattie Ogham walked over.

"That was my pa just rode out," she said flatly. "Gone to tell Clyde what you done. You'll pay, both of you. You'll never get out of the Devil's Kitchen alive."

CHAPTER 11

MATTIE WAS SITTING ON THE PORCH WHEN Clyde Bohannon rode hell-for-leather into the basin, Pop Ogham and Shad Mowry in tow. Clyde pulled savagely on the reins and dismounted on the run. His horse, lathered from stem to stern, its sides billowing, started staggering across the hardpack in the direction of the water troughs, but Mowry caught it up and held it back. The horse was too jiggered to fight.

Clyde charged straight at Mattie, and she yelped surprise as he swept her to her feet.

"Where's Jack?"

"You're hurting me!" she snapped. He was gripping her by the shoulders—gripping so hard that his knuckles were white.

"Where's Jack?"

"Dead. Gone."

"Dead?" Clyde let her go and took a shaky step back, as though she had struck him across the face.

Mattie glared at her father. Pop Ogham was trying to dismount, and all but fell off the saddleless horse. He pressed both hands against the small of his back, wincing. Unaccustomed to riding bareback, he was hurting something fierce. His spine felt as bent and twisted as a cedar post.

"You didn't tell him what happened?" she asked, sharp and accusatory.

"I didn't know iffen Jack was dead or not," said Ogham defensively.

"Well he is," said Mattie, irritable. "Dead as last Sunday's sage hen."

"Who did it?" asked Clyde.

"A man called Slater."

"Sam Slater?"

"Slater. That's all I know." She could tell the name had a strong effect on Clyde.

"Who's he?" queried Ogham. "A tin star?"

"Bounty hunter," muttered Clyde. "Best in the business."

"Some call him The Regulator," commented Mowry. As usual, his dark, hooded eyes were fastened on Mattie.

"How many were there?" Clyde asked Mattie.

"Three. Slater, a woman, and another man. The other man is dead. Jack shot daylight through him. Slater and the woman buried him over yonder."

She pointed, but Clyde didn't bother looking. He stood with fists clenched and shoulders bunched, staring moodily at his boots.

"They rode out about six hours ago," added Mattie. "Took Jack's racer and Bill Lukan's horse."

"Sam Slater," muttered Clyde. "I'm gonna rid the ground of that bastard's shadow."

"You'll need help doing that job," remarked Mowry.

Clyde whirled. "You sayin' we can't get it done?"

"What do you mean, we? I'm not going after Slater."

"The hell you ain't, if I say."

"Doesn't matter what you say. Wasn't my brother he killed. I just resigned from what's left of the Bohannon gang."

Clyde's face darkened. His hand hovered perilously close to his holstered sidegun. Mowry sat easily in his saddle. He didn't look at all the worse for wear after the hard ride from Crow Seep. And he didn't look the least bit worried about handling Clyde should their differences result in gunplay.

"I don't need your help anyhow," growled Clyde, easing off. "Where the hell are you sneakin' off to?"

This last was addressed to Pop Ogham, who had discreetly removed himself from the line of fire, and was now trying to steal into the cabin without being noticed.

"Hell," whimpered Ogham. "My throat's dry as pocket dust, Clyde. I was just gonna fetch a jug, is all."

"Make it quick. We're going after Slater."

"Jesus, Clyde. It's damn near dark and our horses are bottomed out."

Clyde looked up at the darkening sky. The sun had dipped beneath the red rimrock, and early stars were twinkling into life. Gray shadows of night were congregating in the canyon. He seemed surprised, as though until this moment he had not realized the lateness of the hour.

"All right," he said. "We'll leave at dawn. But you'll be riding with me, Pop, and I don't want to hear any lip from you."

"Sure, Clyde."

"Soon as we figure which way they're going, I'll want you to break off and pick up some extra guns. Stony Brown and Apache Joe are holed up at the Roost. John Buck and Three Fingers Smith and a couple others are camped down at Big Water."

"Whatever you say, Clyde."

Ogham's mewling assent apparently did not satisfy Clyde; he lashed out and grabbed a handful of Pop's sweat-damp shirt.

"Listen up, Pop, and listen good. Black Jack made me swear I wouldn't never let him be took in. Said he didn't want to be propped up in some open pine box, the bullet holes plugged with candle wax, so's all the fine, decent folks could file past and gawk at his mortal remains. He said it gave him the cold shudders just to think on it. He made me promise, and I aim to keep that promise if it's the last thing I do."

"O-okay Clyde," stammered Ogham.

Clyde let go of the old rewrite man and glared at Mowry, who was watching Mattie.

"What are you doing? Puttin' down roots? I thought you'd quit this outfit."

Mattie thought Mowry was smiling, but she couldn't be certain because of the thick black beard covering his face. Without a word he dropped the reins of Clyde's horse and rode out of the basin slow and easy, putting his back to Clyde and not once looking around. He didn't appear to be worried about Clyde backshooting him.

She watched him until he was out of sight. Until now she hadn't paid Shad Mowry much attention; suddenly she paid him plenty. Clyde had backed down from this dark, quiet, deadly young man, and Clyde had never backed down from anyone that she knew of, except Jack.

She was only vaguely aware of Clyde brushing past her to enter the cabin, and of her father stepping close and repeating her name, his voice pitched low in an urgent whisper.

"Mattie. Mattie, child, did they take the loot?"

"What?"

"Did the bounty hunters take the money?"

She nodded. Ogham grimaced.

"Dang blast the luck! If it weren't for bad luck I'd have none at all."

Morose, he followed Clyde into the cabin. She heard someone fumble with a lamp. Later she heard them shoving a jug of corn liquor back and forth across the rough cedar-pole table. They didn't talk much. She sat down, arms wrapped around drawn-up legs, chin resting on her knees. Staring off into space, she dreamed of pretty dresses and fabulous, far-off places. Night covered the land like a cape of black velvet lined with moon-silver. Lamplight spilled out of the doorway, casting her shadow long across the hardpack. Lost in her thoughts, she was only dimly aware of the snores sounding from the cabin. Clyde and her father had likkered themselves into profound slumber.

"Mattie."

She blinked and looked up to find Shad Mowry standing in front of her. He was watching the doorway, listening to the two men sawing logs.

"I knew you'd come back," she said.

"Did you? You know why?"

"I know. I can tell by the way you been lookin' at me."

"Come with me, Mattie. Ain't nothing for you here. We'll have us a high ol' time, you and me. I'll take good care of you. Better than Black Jack Bohannon ever done."

"He promised to take me places," she said coyly. "To buy me pretty dresses and such."

"I'll buy you all the foofaraw your little heart desires. I got my share of the Hanksville bank job from Clyde when we were down at Crow Seep."

She stood up. "Not enough," she declared flatly.

He watched her, his black eyes glittering like polished obsidian.

"The bounty hunters took the sack of money Jack had with him," she said.

"I'll get it for you if that's what you want, Mattie. Anything you want, girl. Just so long as you come with me."

"They also got Jack's body, which is worth $2,000."

She heard a sound like that of a dog panting, and realized it was Mowry, laughing softly.

"You want to collect the reward on Black Jack," he said, amused by the thought.

"Why, yes," she replied, righteously. "I do indeed. He promised to buy me a pretty dress for every day of the week. I think he ought to keep his promise, don't you?"

"I reckon he will. One way or another."

He went to the corral and saddled one of the horses. When he returned to the porch, Mattie was tiptoeing out of the cabin. She had her Montgomery Ward wishbook under an arm. Mowry listened carefully to the measured rhythm of the snoring from within as she mounted up. Satisfied that Clyde and Ogham were dead to the world, he walked out of the basin, leading Mattie's horse, making for the spot down-canyon where he had left his own cayuse.

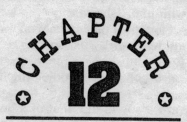

CHAPTER 12

SLATER FIGURED BOHANNON HAD PICKED THE best way into the Devil's Kitchen after the Hanksville robbery. Consequently, the best way out was to backtrack. Down the canyons, across the rocky tableland, and through the sand hills he rode with Miss Bounty and three dead outlaws. He led the horse over which the body of Black Jack was draped. Rachel rode the other horse, with the Lukan brothers in tow, belly-down over the mules.

Towing their grisly cargo slowed them down, and sunset caught them shy of the Swope homestead, out in the open on the high slickrock, where by reading the sign, Slater judged the posse had lost the outlaw gang's trail sometime yesterday.

"This isn't a good place to stop," commented Rachel. "No cover."

"Thanks for telling me."

"What are partners for?"

Slater turned the canelo off the trail he had been following all afternoon. "Come on."

"You lead and I'll follow, like the good, little woman I am."

"Right. Just keep an eye on our backtrail."

"Of course. Don't you trust me?"

Slater didn't waste breath answering that question.

Bouncing against his leg was a gunnysack filled with money, tied off to his saddlehorn. He knew Mattie Ogham was right: Black Jack's brother Clyde would certainly be after them, and with as many of the Devil's Kitchen longriders as he could get his hands on. Clyde would be motivated by revenge, certainly, but no less by greed. Twelve thousand dollars had been taken from the Hanksville bank, and though he hadn't spent precious time counting the money in the sack, Slater guessed that at least half the loot was now in his possession.

He remembered this part of the Kitchen from the weeks spent tracking the elusive Slick Owens, and now he led the way between a pair of small rock buttes, through a side draw, and into another serpentine canyon. The sulfur smell of water heavily impregnated with gypsum excited the animals, and they quickened their gait.

A half mile farther on, the canyon widened to

host a flat table of bunchgrass. A pool of reddish water was trapped between the north wall of the canyon and the edge of the flat, nourished by a spring trickling out of the wall fifty feet overhead. Green rushes and wild roses grew thick around the pool, and the soft evening breeze rustled the gray-green leaves of a dusty cottonwood clinging tenaciously to the base of the canyon wall. Out in the grass on the flat, cottontails scattered in panic at their approach, and an unseen rattler crossly sounded its ominous warning.

Rachel coughed at the bitter sting of gypsum in the dust, an indiscretion sharply magnified as the sound echoed off the sheer red and yellow shanks of the canyon. The brush around the pool thrashed and crackled, and an old steer burst into the open. The mossback gave them a jaundiced look, then broke into a shambling run across the flat.

"Slow elk," said Slater, smiling faintly as he glanced at Rachel—and at the gun in her hand.

"You wouldn't give me my own gun back," she said, "so I took one from the cabin."

"I know."

"You didn't expect me to travel across the Devil's Kitchen without a weapon, did you? And what do you mean, you knew?"

"I knew you were carrying."

Rachel was skeptical. She wore a man's shirt over the ruined upper portion of her dress, belted at the waist with a length of hard-twist. The shirt fit very loosely, and she found it hard to believe that

Slater could have known for certain about the revolver concealed beneath it. She chided herself for having let the *cimarrone* spook her into drawing the gun.

As the animals drank, she made to dismount, and Slater waited until she touched ground to say, "You'll be sorry if you drink that."

She took a near-empty canteen from her saddle. "I've learned to take what I can get."

"There's sweet water just up ahead."

She gave him a sour look, hung the canteen by its strap on the saddlehorn, and remounted. "You know this country pretty well."

"Well enough."

"They say you're part Apache."

"I lived with them. They took me in—adopted me."

"Your parents, what happened to them?"

"Killed."

"Mine, too." Rachel scanned the high rimrock, where windswept spires and ledges were touched by the last light of the dying day. "They were murdered by Arkansas Tom Claver and the Yuma Kid."

"Outlaws?"

"Yes. But at the time they'd hired their guns to Jubal Allred, the rancher. Allred had a small army of gunslingers on the payroll. Their orders were to clean out squatters. That's what they called my folks, and others like them, who staked legal claim to free soil that Allred thought he owned just because he'd been grazing his cattle there for twenty years. Claver and the Kid shot my folks down in cold blood, and they raped me. They should have killed me. That's what Claver said, right before I blew his head off with a shotgun at full choke."

"That how you got started in this business?"

She nodded. "I've killed Arkansas Tom and the Kid a dozen times each." She looked sharply at him, her emerald-green eyes glittering in the gray twilight. "Doesn't make any sense to you, does it?"

"Sure. Revenge."

"You could say that."

Slater recalled how she had stood, calm and in control, while the Lukan brothers manhandled her. That couldn't have been easy, he decided, after what Claver and the Yuma Kid had done to her years ago. And all that talk about how she bedded down with an outlaw before killing him made sense, in a twisted way.

"Let's ride," he said.

They did not proceed much farther down the canyon before turning up a steep side draw. A hundred yards later, the draw seemed to be blocked by two immense slabs of sandstone fallen from the cliff above. Catclaw grew densely here. It looked like a dead end to Rachel, but Slater dismounted and led his horse and the one carrying Bohannon forward, so she, too, stepped down and followed, dragging the ornery knobheads behind her.

Slater found a narrow game trail snaking through the catclaw. Prickly branches lashed at her clothing and hair, but Rachel pushed resolutely on, and in moments saw the tunnel. It was just a space, shaped like an inverted V, beneath the slabs of rock wedged against one another, scarcely large enough for a horse to squeak through.

On the other side of the slabs, the draw flattened out and opened up. Here more catclaw grew around a cave entrance. Ground-hitching the horses and mules, they entered the cave. Water seeped down the slick walls and dripped from cracks in the ceiling thirty feet overhead. The floor of the cave was wet and slippery. Slater knelt and scooped sand out of a shallow depression in the stone. In minutes the depression had filled with water.

Rachel knelt, cupped her hands and drank. The water was cold and sweet. She gratefully laved her face and neck. Slater sat on his heels and watched, his features impassive.

"Like what you see?" she asked, a challenge in her tone of voice.

He stood and left the cave. She watched him go, speculatively, then shrugged and unbuttoned her shirt. Splashing water on her breasts and belly, she wondered if she could wash away the memory of the Lukans' rough hands.

Suddenly he was standing there in front of her, and she saw the .32 Savage in his hand. He offered the gun.

"This mean we're partners?" she asked, with that quirky half-smile.

"No. It means I'm tired of lugging all this hardware around. The Bible's in my saddlebags, if you want it."

She took the gun. "If the money gets too heavy for you, Slater, I'll be more than happy to carry it, too."

"Belongs to the Farmers & Merchants Bank."

"Jesus, Slater. Ease up a little. I know that. Where's your sense of humor? After what I told you, do you honestly think I do this for money?"

"I don't know what to think about you."

She rose, and didn't bother buttoning the shirt. He could see her breasts, pale globes of firm, white flesh in the incomplete darkness.

Rachel Myers was a very desirable woman, no question. Miss Bounty, indeed! Despite what some people said, Slater was human. Occasionally he needed what all men needed—the complete fulfillment that only a woman could bring to a man. Right now he wanted to see what the rest of Rachel Myers looked like, what she felt like; the devil take the cost.

"What's the matter?" she asked, her voice a husky whisper. "Don't you trust me?"

"You keep asking me that. The answer's no."

"Well, you don't have to trust me to make love to me, do you?"

"Why?"

She stepped closer. Her arms curled like velvet snakes around his neck.

"Why not?"

As he pulled her roughly against him and crushed her lips with his own, he wondered if this meant she was going to have to kill him come morning.

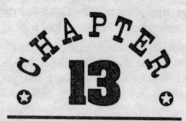

CHAPTER 13

SLATER SLEPT IN BRIEF SNATCHES THAT night. The slightest sound brought him awake and alert, as did the smallest movement by the woman who lay beside him. The blanket beneath him was damp, having soaked up water from the wet stone on the cave floor. The cave itself became quite cool as the night wore on. He didn't mind at all, after the blistering and breathless heat of yesterday; tomorrow promised to be another dose of hell.

In the early morning hours the coyotes came to investigate the blanket-wrapped bundles lined up outside the cave entrance. The horses whickered nervously and a mule brayed. Slater pulled on his pants and slipped out of the cave to drive the scavengers away. He knew from past experience that coyotes frequented this spring. They fed on the berries of the profuse catclaw, disgorging the seeds in stringy clots.

He hauled the bundles farther into the cave. The bodies were stiff, the blankets splotched with dried blood. The coyotes returned, and a couple sat in the cave entrance, keeping the horses and mules restless. Slater shook his head. Coyotes were damned nuisances, bold as brass, and as he could not risk a fire, he took up the Spencer carbine and sat cross-legged at the mouth of the cave until false dawn.

Rachel was awakened by the fluttering wings of a cave swallow. She saw Slater sitting there, his back to her, and a half dozen coyotes arrayed before him, a couple so close that he might have reached out and touched one of them.

"Looks like everybody wants a piece of Black Jack Bohannon," she joked, dressing quickly.

For some time, no other words passed between them. They saddled the horses and strapped the bodies down with rope. Breakfast consisted of hardtack and spring water. Rachel made no mention of last night's intimacy, and Slater was glad of it. No soft endearments. The attraction between them was purely physical, and he wished it to stay that way.

They were about to leave the hidden spring when from the canyon below came the thunder of many horses on the run, the sound bouncing off the steep walls. Slater gestured curtly for Rachel to stay put, and stole through the tunnel beneath the slab rock to get a look. When he returned a moment later the thunder was still echoing off the high reaches.

"Just horses," he said. "Mustangs."

Leaving the hidden spring, they turned west. A haze of dust hung suspended in the still, morning air. The sign of a dozen horses, some shod, went before them. In an hour's time they came upon the wild ones on a grass flat similar to the one they had visited yesterday.

The stallion, a big bucksin, bugled the alarm and led the flight down a side canyon. Slater figured some of the mares had been mockeys from birth, while others were cavvy-broke range plugs stolen by the stallion from the herds of area ranches. The stallion no doubt knew this maze of canyons, draws, and hidden valleys better than any man. The Devil's Kitchen was haven to outlaw horses as well as lawless men.

The canyon narrowed beyond the flat. A mad jumble of boulders decorated the steep slopes. A premonition of danger triggered a reflex precaution in Slater. He thumbed the holster's leather thong off the Schofield's hammer. Ice-blue eyes scanned both slopes. He didn't see anything to warrant concern, but long years of hard-won experience enabled him to recognize first-rate ambush ground when he saw it.

He glanced over his shoulder at Rachel. She was looking skyward, and he followed her gaze. Buzzards flew in lazy circles in the brass-colored sky. The only sound was the raspy breathing of the horses and mules, the creak of saddle leather, the unavoidable clatter of steelshod hooves on stone.

And then—another sound. A telltale trickle of rock rubble somewhere on the leftside slope. Slater looked that way, and in the next heartbeat saw the flash of sun on a gunbarrel.

Rachel saw it, too, and her sharp-spoken warning coincided with the thunderclap of a rifleshot. Slater felt the burn of a bullet graze across his back above the left shoulder blade. He bent forward and slipped sideways out of the saddle. His left leg hooked the cantle, and his left hand gripped the pommel. In this way he clung to the right side of the horse, shielded by the canelo's bulk. Drawing the Schofield, he fired from underneath the animal's neck, his gun arm braced against the horse's chest.

More gunfire erupted from the barranca's south slope. Slater's first impression was that there were perhaps a half-dozen drygulchers up there, certianly no more, and that part of him which remained coolly analytical in crisis wondered why the ambushers had failed to occupy both flanks of the canyon.

A first impression was all he had time for. The horse bearing Bohannon's corpse was tied with rope to his saddlehorn. As the canelo lunged forward, Bohannon's horse balked and locked its forelegs. Slater felt the lead rope go taut as fiddle-string beneath his left leg, costing him his anchor on the cantle. In the same instant he felt the canelo shudder and stumble, and knew, with a sick feeling, that his horse had been hit. The canelo pitched sideways. Slater let go and tried to jump clear.

He almost made it. The dead weight of the falling horse struck him behind the legs and pitched him to the ground. Slater ate dust. A slug scorched the breathless heat and screamed off rock, throwing splinters into his face, gashing his cheek. *That's all I need,* he thought. *Another scar.*

Rolling, he sat up and fanned the Schofield's hammer, sending five rounds into the rocks. Without a definite target he could only hope to keep their attackers' heads down until he could find cover.

An endless drumroll of gun thunder hammered the barranca. Rachel rid herself of the lead ropes and cast loose the mules bearing the bodies of the Lukan brothers. She goaded her mount forward and came alongside the horse carrying Bohannon, anchored by its own lead rope to the saddle of the canelo. She grabbed the rope, and sunlight flashed off the blade of the clasp knife in her other hand. Slater had no idea where she had gotten the knife, and he didn't have the time to ask.

Cutting the lead rope, she kicked her horse into a high lope, the horse carrying Bohannon in tow. The mules followed. Realizing a little too late what Rachel was up to, Slater got up and started running after her. Hot lead scorched the air and shimmied off rock all around. Veering right, he sought cover in a pile of boulders at the base of the north slope.

He thought that just maybe the bushwhackers

would concentrate their fire on Rachel, now that he wasn't such a target. Plucking bullets from his gunbelt, he filled the Schofield as quickly as he could, but even then Rachel was out of range. Slater cursed his luck. In spite of what had happened between them last night, he would have killed her without second thought. After all, she was making off with Black Jack Bohannon and leaving him to the mercy of the ambushers—mercy which, in all likelihood, didn't exist.

The bushwhackers weren't able to stop her, either, not that they didn't try. Slater began to think he was pitted against men who weren't very good shots. Small consolation.

Fading hoofbeats signaled Rachel's successful escape. The gunfire diminished. A couple of bullets came winging into the pile of boulders sheltering Slater, but he didn't return fire. No point wasting ammunition. He couldn't hope to reach them with a handgun, and his carbine lay under 900 pounds of dead horse.

Checking the north slope above him, he quickly concluded that to try gaining higher ground would expose him to enemy fire. Maybe they weren't sharpshooters, but men had been killed by lucky shots before.

The best he could do, then, was wait it out. One of three things would happen. They might decide to come for him, at least some of them, in which case he could make them regret venturing within handgun range, or they would pursue Rachel, some or all of them, and at the very least the odds against him would be reduced; or they would sit up there all day, hoping he was foolish enough to show himself. If that proved to be their plan, he could wait for nightfall and slip away.

But just this once, Slater's patience failed him. Problem was, Rachel Myers was getting away with $2,000 that rightfully belonged to him. That really rubbed against his grain. If he waited very long, Miss Bounty would get clean away. Slater was not inclined to let that happen.

So he couldn't afford to wait for night, or for the ambushers to come for him. He had to take the battle to the enemy. He had to flush them out of those rocks, the way a bird dog flushed quail out of shinnery. He had to cross fifty yards of open ground to get to the other slope, where he would work his way up through the jumbled rocks and kill them one by one.

The decision made, Slater wasted no more time. He burst into the open, straight into a storm of rifle fire, and answered with his own blazing gun.

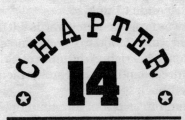

•CHAPTER•
14

"CHRIST!" BREATHED WHITMORE, THOR-
oughly disgusted. "That bastard is hard to kill."

Crouched in the rocks a hundred feet below the
barranca's southern rim, he glanced down at the lit-
ter of empty shell casings around him. He realized
with dismay that he had spent thirty rounds. The
other members of the Hanksville posse had pretty
much matched him in this respect, and all they had
managed to kill was Slater's cinnamon-colored
horse.

Whitmore's rifle was a Winchester Model 1873,
chambered to take revolver shells. Now, groping at
his gunbelt for fresh loads, he was shocked to find
all the leather loops empty. Panic rising in him, he
frisked himself, and found a few .44's in his shirt

pocket. Did he have any extra ammunition in his possibles? He didn't think so.

McVey was crouched a few yards left of his position; Bryner and Stoddard were fifteen, maybe twenty, yards to his right. Whitmore couldn't see the T Anchor hired hand or the Hanksville gunsmith, so he turned back to McVey.

"I'm damn near out of ammunition," he said.

McVey nodded. "If we can kill Slater, we can take his."

"I thought you were some kind of gun artist," snapped Whitmore, his tone accusatory.

McVey kept his attention glued to the boulder-strewn slope below. Slater was somewhere down there, having made it across the open ground from the other side of the narrow canyon—somehow. Privately, McVey could scarcely believe he had failed to bring the manhunter down, and his confidence in his abilities was severely shaken, but he had no intention of admitting as much to Whitmore.

He knew perfectly well what Whitmore was implying. Whitmore knew he was all big talk now, so he *had* to kill Slater. Sure, he was afraid of the bounty hunter. A man would have to be plumb loco not to be scared of Slater. It was quite possible that Slater would kill him instead, but he was less afraid of dying than he was of failing to live up to his reputation. It was a reputation built on the shaky foundation of gross exaggerations and downright falsehoods, but it was the only reputation he had, and he nurtured it jealously.

The scrape of bootheels on rock spun him around—Whitmore too—and Stoddard came perilously close to being shot full of holes. The Hanksville gunsmith ducked down beside Whitmore.

"Wonder if one of those bodies was Bohannon," said Stoddard.

Whitmore had been wondering the same thing. "We've got to catch her. How do you stand with ammunition?"

Stoddard shook his head. "If bullets were beans I'd starve to death."

"Where did the woman come from anyway?" asked McVey.

"I'd swear that was the sister we seen a few days back," replied the gunsmith, whose eyesight was sharper than most men's. "You know, the one that was traveling with the preacher man."

"I'll be damned," muttered Whitmore. "Means she isn't a psalm-singer after all, and that wasn't a preacher, either. I'll bet they were goddamned bounty hunters."

"There he is!" yelled McVey.

They all began firing wildly into the rocks below. Whitmore expended several more precious rounds before realizing he hadn't actually seen anything worth shooting at. His heart felt like it was going to explode out of his chest. He cursed himself mercilessly. He was too afraid to think straight.

"Did we get him?" he asked, hoping against hope.

"Hell, no," replied McVey.

"He's just one man," Whitmore growled, trying to convince himself as well as the others. "I say we go down there and finish it."

"You're crazy," said McVey. "Better to wait and let him come to us."

"That so-called sister is getting away with Bohannon."

"After this, I don't fancy leaving Slater alive," admitted Stoddard miserably.

"Right," said McVey. "He'll come for you sooner or later. Best end it here."

"God—how did we get into this mess?" whined Stoddard.

"We've got to be the ones who take Bohannon in," insisted Whitmore.

"Go get him if it means so much to you," said McVey. "Leave Slater to me."

Whitmore was skeptical. "You sound pretty sure of yourself."

McVey was happy to hear that, because he didn't feel sure at all. But if he somehow managed to kill Sam Slater he would finally have a real reputation. He could envision walking down a street and men crossing to the other side to keep out of his way. And when he strolled into a saloon they'd make plenty of space for him at the bar. They would buy him drinks; he would never have to buy his own whiskey again. And if a wet-behind-the-ears pilgrim who fancied himself a gunhawk just because he could knock six tin cans off six fence posts with six shots even contemplated calling him out, men in the know would warn him not to tangle with the shootist who had killed The Regulator.

That was the kind of life worth dying for.

"Go on," he urged, these visions giving him a fresh dose of courage. He didn't want to share the glory with them, and he didn't want them to see him fail. "Go on and get Bohannon's carcass. I don't care about the reward. I never did. Money ain't why I come this far."

"I don't want the reward either," snapped Whitmore. "At least not for myself. Don't forget, I've got a sheriff's badge in my pocket that had better be found in Bohannon's, or we'll all hang."

"Sure. We'll all hang for what *you* did."

"Come on, George," hissed Stoddard urgently. He was past ready to put miles between himself and Slater. "If he wants to try it alone, for God's sake let him."

Whitmore glowered at McVey a moment, then nodded curtly.

"Go tell Bryner," he said to Stoddard. "I'll meet the two of you on the rim."

McVey kept his attention and rifle trained on the rocks below while the others clambered up through the boulders to the rim. He was hoping Slater would stick his neck out and try to get a shot at Whitmore or one of the others.

His mouth was dust-dry, his palms sweaty. All through life he had bragged and swaggered, talking himself up, how tough he was, how he was not one to be messed with, even to the point of believing it himself. He had, in essence, talked himself into it. Now he had to see it through, the devil take the cost.

He heard someone coming down through the rocks behind him, and grimaced, unwilling to take his eyes off the slope below, for fear of missing his one chance at Slater.

"I said I'd handle him," he muttered crossly. "Get the hell on, will you? I don't need your help."

"I didn't come to help, exactly," said Slater.

Blood run cold, McVey whirled. Slater grabbed the barrel of the rifle as it came around, pulled and twisted all at once, wrenching the weapon from McVey's grasp and throwing McVey off balance. As McVey stumbled forward, he collided with Slater's fist. Next he knew, he was flat on his back in a world of pain.

Leaning the rifle against a slab of rock, Slater bent, got a fistful of shirt, and lifted McVey clean off the ground with contemptuous ease. He slammed the gunhawk against a boulder and stepped in close, holstering the Schofield.

"Is this what you want?" he asked, the words hissing through clenched teeth, his tone as soft and deadly as the tread of an Apache bronco.

McVey's face was ghastly white.

"Here's your big chance," said Slater harshly. "You wanted to try your luck with Bohannon. He's dead. You'll have to settle for me. So let's finish it here and now, face-to-face. Man to man. I've got to kill you. No choice. I can't turn my back on you."

McVey tried to say something. He wasn't able

to get it past the lump in his throat. Just as well; he thought he had enough grit to tell Slater to go to hell, but he wasn't absolutely certain he wouldn't have begged for his life instead.

"You can't miss at this range," said Slater.

He still had McVey by the shirtfront, pressing him against the rough red flank of the boulder. They were an arm's length apart. He could smell McVey's fear. He watched McVey's eyes. A split-second before McVey slapped leather, those eyes telegraphed the move. Slater had the Schofield drawn before McVey could clear either Colt Lightning from its holster. Driving the Schofield into McVey's belly at an upward angle, he pulled the trigger.

The report was muffled. McVey jackknifed forward. Slater let him go and stepped back. The Colts clattered on stone as McVey pitched facedown, a blood-splattered boulder his tombstone.

Slater holstered the Schofield again, retrieved the rifle, and headed for the rim, after what was left of the Hanksville posse.

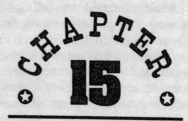

•CHAPTER•
15

REACHING THE RIM, WHITMORE AND THE
other two Hanksville men turned west, making for
the draw where their horses were cached.

Following the night attack on what had turned
out to be the Moab posse, they had tried without
success to find the slickrock where they had lost the
Bohannon gang's trail. The next course of action decided upon had been relocating the Swope homestead and working from there. This had turned
them west toward the Sunset Rim, and ultimately
into this canyon.

The sound of horses had driven them up into
the draw and then onto the barranca's southern ex-
posure with ambush in mind. The horses they had
heard were the mustangs, but they had no way of

knowing that. Seeing Slater, Whitmore had decided his luck had finally changed.

Now he wasn't so sure. When they heard the single gunshot, and Stoddard looked back hopefully, Whitmore simply grimaced and shook his head. In his studied opinion, McVey stood no chance against Slater, and he seriously doubted one shot was enough to kill the bounty hunter. He expected the worst.

This outlook was made manifest to the others when, upon reaching the draw, Whitmore mounted up and grabbed hold of the reins on McVey's horse.

"You're taking his horse?" asked Bryner.

"What does it look like?"

"You can't do that," said Stoddard, without conviction.

"Watch me."

"You can't leave him in here on foot."

"He's buzzard bait by now. You want to leave this horse for Slater? Is that what you want?"

Stoddard anxiously scanned the rim they had just quit.

"You can wait to see which one comes down out of those rocks if you want to," said Whitmore, prodding his horse into motion, leading McVey's mount.

The Hanksville gunsmith turned his own horse and followed Whitmore and the T Anchor range rider.

Next he knew, he was lying on the rocky ground, feeling as though someone had taken a fence post and knocked him out of the saddle with it. Stunned, he realized his right side was completely numb from the waist up, and looked to see the blood soaking his shirt high up on the right shoulder. Nausea swept over him. He'd been shot! He tried to call out for help, but what burst from his lips was an incoherent yelp.

Whitmore and Bryner fired up into the rocks. Once again, Whitmore didn't see anything to shoot at. Stoddard's horse clattered past, trotting down the draw. Whitmore glanced back and saw the gunsmith sprawled on the ground. He was alive, writhing. The civilized thing to do was to go back and help him, but the civilized thing took courage. Like his ammunition, Whitmore had spent just about all the courage he had in his possession.

As he pointed his horse down the draw, he heard Bryner yell after him. The T Anchor man sounded angry. Whitmore didn't look back.

Bryner *was* angry—angry and scared—scared of Sam Slater and death, which were pretty much one and the same. He was angry at Whitmore; the man who all along had insisted they stick together apparently believed now that it was every man for himself.

The T Anchor range rider wanted to go back for Stoddard, but he also wanted to stay alive. For a handful of precious seconds he sat his pivoting horse, trying to make the most important decision of his young life. Then, bracing himself, he got his horse under control and started back for the wounded gunsmith.

Dismounting, reins gripped tightly, he knelt beside Stoddard and for an anxious moment thought the gunsmith was dead. But Stoddard, passed out, was still breathing shallowly.

A shadow passed across Bryner. His first thought was that a buzzard had swooped low to check the menu. He looked up to find Slater standing over him. Bryner shuddered. Suddenly remembering the gun in his hand, he started to raise it. Slater swept McVey's rifle into line.

"Live or die," said the bounty hunter.

It didn't sound to Bryner like Slater much cared which way he went.

The T Anchor cowboy tossed the six-gun away. Slater pulled the reins out of Bryner's hand.

"I'm obliged for the loan of your horse."

"You done for him," said Bryner dully, looking at Stoddard, at all the blood.

"He's not finished."

"I heard you tell Sheriff Elledge you only killed for money. Guess that was wrong."

"How's that? You're all outlaws in my book. You hanged an innocent man, remember? When the word got out, you'd all be wanted. You could say I'm getting an early start on hunting you down."

Bryner started to voice protest, but clamped his mouth tightly shut. Slater was right all the way. He had entered the Devil's Kitchen an honest man on an honorable mission. Somehow things had gone terribly wrong. It was like a bad dream. He wanted to blame Whitmore, wanted to explain to Slater that

Whitmore had talked them into hanging Swope, that it was Whitmore who had backshot the Moab sheriff, Will Ashley. But he couldn't, because he knew he was as much to blame as Whitmore, and that a man was alone accountable for his own actions. No excuse was legitimate, no circumstance mitigating.

"So you're going to take me in," said Bryner, resigned to his fate, feeling he deserved what was bound to happen. "Belly-down over my horse, right? Isn't that your style? Dead man's ride."

"Maybe I would, except I only got the one horse."

"You would have killed me, had I run away like Whitmore."

Slater's features were dark and impassive.

"For the horse. Nothing personal."

Bryner sat back on his heels. Taking wheatstraw paper and a muslin pouch of Lone Jack, he built a smoke. He offered the makings to Slater, who declined with a curt headshake. The cowboy's hands shook slightly.

He realized now that his decision to turn back and help Stoddard, rather than to flee like Whitmore, had saved his bacon. He couldn't say how or why he knew this, but Slater would not have let him live had he made the wrong choice. It wasn't just about the horse. Somehow, to some degree, he had redeemed himself in Slater's eyes.

He lit a strike-anywhere and fired the quirly, squinting speculatively at Slater through the biting blue smoke. The bounty hunter was hunkered down in horse shade, not six feet away.

"So what do I do?" asked the cowboy.

Slater glanced at Stoddard. "See to him. Bullet passed clean through the shoulder. If you can stop the bleeding he'll make it."

"I wasn't the one pistol-whipped you, Slater. For what it's worth."

"Where's Ricker?"

"Dead."

To Bryner's amazement, Slater did not ask for details.

"Ride out of this country, Bryner."

Bryner nodded. "Obliged."

Slater rose, untied the lass-rope from Bryner's saddle and let it fall to the ground.

"There's a band of wild horses somewhere east of here," he said, realizing that the passage of the mustangs through the canyon had obliterated the sign of the Hanksville men, which in turn was the reason he had blundered like a greenhorn into ambush. "Some of the mares are cavvy-broke. Get a loop on one of 'em, you won't have to work too many kinks out of her back."

Bryner didn't speak. Slater stepped up into the saddle.

"Make sure we don't meet again, Bryner."

The T Anchor hand nodded again, eyes downcast.

Slater spun the horse around and rode away.

CHAPTER 16

IT WAS GETTING ON TOWARD SUNSET WHEN Pop Ogham kicked, cursed and cajoled his tired horse through Kiowa Notch and along a high mountain ledge to a bench thick with scrub juniper and snakeweed. The ledge was the only access to the place known by the outlaw brotherhood of the Devil's Kitchen as The Roost.

Built beneath a ledge was a rock house with an adjoining corral. Pop had spent most of his adult life in the Kitchen, and he didn't know who had built the house way up here, or why. As long as he could remember, it had been used as a hideout by local desperadoes.

Pop was dead tired. He ached miserably from his second full day of hard riding. In younger years he could have spent an entire week, day and night, in the saddle, and often had, trailing stolen cattle through hidden valleys by moonlight. Getting old was a pain. A good long draw on a jug of corn liquor would work wonders. He'd been stone sober entirely too long.

His horse whickered sharply, sidestepping so abruptly that Pop, caught unawares, almost pitched out of the saddle. His curse died stillborn as a man stepped out of the shinnery. The man had a sawed-off shotgun hooked nonchalantly under one arm. Dressed in range clothes, he wore a red headband in place of a hat. His features were broad and dark, his lank hair almost completely gray.

"Get down," said the man gruffly.

"Filthy savage," muttered Pop, who knew the man as Apache Joe.

The scattergun came up.

"Drunken fool," retorted Apache Joe.

He wasn't Apache at all. Part Yaqui, part Pima, he had been cast out long ago by his own kind, and for the past forty years had diligently practiced a particularly brutal form of banditry. He was a highwayman, and he sometimes killed his victims whether they cooperated or not. He usually worked alone, and it was little wonder, mused Pop. The murderous old copperbelly was half-crazy. When local women tried to scare their children into living right, they substituted Apache Joe for the boogey man. Pop personally thought Joe's cinch was loose on account of too much peyote.

"I've come with a message from Clyde Bohannon," announced Ogham, dismounting. "Where's Stony Brown?"

Apache Joe nodded sideways, indicating the rock house. Pop trudged in that direction, wondering for the thousandth time what he had gotten himself into. He was flat worried. For many a year he had successfully plied his trade as a livestock thief and rewrite man, always playing it safe, keeping a low profile, staying out of scrapes. Now here he was, Clyde Bohannon's errand boy, involved in a dangerous game that he was wholly unprepared and utterly unfit to partake in.

He was worried, too, for his daughter. Mattie had slipped away last night, and by the sign he and Clyde had tried to read the next morning, in spite of bust-head hangovers, it was clear she hadn't slipped away alone. Clyde had guessed that Shad Mowry was the culprit. Pop morosely shook his head as he neared the rock house, Apache Joe catfooting along behind. Like all women, Mattie was difficult, if not impossible, to figure out. Black Jack not long dead, and here she was running off with another owlhoot.

Three men emerged from the rock house and fanned out. The man in the middle was a small, bandy-legged character with a scraggly beard hanging halfway down his shirt front and a head as bald and smooth as a baby's bottom. With his big, hooked nose and bulging eyes, he looked like a bird of prey.

This was Stony Brown. With Black Jack gone, Pop figured Stony qualified as the big screw among the Kitchen's outlaw bunch. He was smart, mean, and an old hand at the game.

It was Stony who had introduced a number of now established techniques to the increasingly popular pastime of train holdups. Stony was the first to think of uncoupling the engine and express car and moving them some distance up the track from the rest of the train. And it was Stony who dreamed up the little trick of driving a herd of horses into the area just prior to a robbery, and then using the herd to confuse the sign he and his cohorts made during the getaway.

"Howdy, Pop," said Stony, with a free and easy attitude that didn't fool Pop Ogham for a second. "What brings you up this high?"

"Clyde Bohannon sent me to fetch you."

"Yeah?" Stony glanced at the two men beside him, looking greatly amused. "I didn't know we was part and parcel of the Bohannon gang. Did you all know that, boys? Did you know that when one of the Bohannons snapped their fingers we jumped?"

"Not what I meant to say," said Ogham contritely. "Black Jack's dead. Clyde needs your help to get the man who did it."

"Black Jack Bohannon's dead?" Stony tugged fiercely on his beard. "Well don't that beat all? Who's the hardcase managed that?"

"Sam Slater."

DALE ✪ COLTER

One of the other men rolled a mangled cigar from one side of his mouth to the other. "Figures."

Pop recognized him as John Buck, the Texas gunslinger. Buck, like Charley Siringo, had started out a cowpuncher, graduating to lawman and gambler. Unlike Siringo, his quick temper, quicker gun, and nonexistent scruples had pushed him, little by little, into stepping over the fine line that separated the law-abiding from the lawless.

"I heard you were down on the Big Water, John," said Pop.

"Come to pay a social call and shoot some breeze," was the drawling reply. "Me and Three Fingers were gettin' sick and tired of just each other for company."

The man on the other side of Stony Brown was clad head to toe in grimy buckskins. Pop could scarcely see his face for all the hair. Many winters ago, Three Fingers Smith had been a mountain man. He'd lost one finger on his right hand in a bear trap and a second to a Blackfoot knife. He was a dead shot with his old Hawken.

"Where's Clyde now?" asked Stony.

"Trailing Slater. He figures you could meet him at the Swope place by noon tomorrow, and then ya'll could catch Slater past the Sunset Rim, out in the open, before he could get anywhere near Hanksville."

Again Stony glanced at John Buck and Three Fingers. Then he motioned Apache Joe over and flashed a big, yellow-toothed smile at Pop that made Ogham awful nervous.

"Me and the boys'll have a little parley, Pop. 'Scuse us for half a smoke."

Pop waited while Stony and the others stepped into the rock house. He watched them by the light of a bitch lamp inside, standing just within the door with their heads together. Instinct for self-preservation, finely developed over several decades of nightriding, began working on him, and the soles of his feet began itching something fierce. Pop knew what that meant. Time to dust out. He'd done what Clyde had wanted him for, so why in blue blazes was he standing here like a storefront Indian?

He was turning to fit boot to stirrup when Stony and the others came out into the twilight gloom. The others dallied around the rock house while Stony waddled over.

"What's your hurry, Pop?" asked Stony, in that dubiously affable manner of his.

"I done what Clyde wanted. Reckon I'll go on to home."

"Well, Pop, we got a proposition for you."

A proposition from Stony Brook and company was the last thing Pop wanted to hear, but he was afraid that to say so would be impolite. Stony was the kind of man you always made a point of being polite to.

"What kind of proposition?"

"Well, we recollect ol' Black Jack's worth about 2,000 simoleons in reward money. We also heard tell the Bohannon gang took nigh on $10,000 out of that Hanksville bank."

"Closer to twelve."

"Who's got the loot, Pop?"

"Clyde's got some of it. I reckon Slater's carryin' about half. Shad Mowry quit the outfit and rode off with his share." *And my only daughter*, thought Pop. *Damn his eyes.*

"What about the Lukans?"

"Dead."

"Well I'll be." Stony grinned like a coyote just back from the chicken coop. "Pop, you know me. I don't like to take the long way around nothin'. I'm partial to straight talk. Me and the boys were thinkin' about holdin' up the Pacific & El Paso's Lightning Express. The army ships payroll by the Express. Problem is, they ship a squad of yellow-leg soldier boys along with it, so it ain't exactly what you might call easy pickings."

"You mean you ain't gonna help Clyde?"

"Don't mean no such, Pop. We'll go along and help him settle Sam Slater's hash, sure enough. And then we aim to settle Clyde's."

Pop felt a funny tingle at the base of his spine, and knew it was that yellow streak breaking out again.

"You aim to doublecross Clyde?"

Stony nodded. "That's the long and short of it. See, that way, we get the Hanksville loot. We also get Black Jack's molderin' carcass. All we have to do then is collect. Strikes us as a sight easier than tangling with soldiers for a payroll. But we've got to find somebody we can trust, somebody who ain't papered, to take Black Jack in and collect the bounty. We just natch'ly thought of you."

"Me?"

"Sure. You're a sly ol' devil, Pop. You've rustled enough cattle and horses to stock a dozen ranches, but you ain't never been caught, far as we know. Never had your face plastered all over a damned wanted poster. None of us could ride into Hanksville, or any other town in the territory. You could pull it off, though."

"I dunno, Stony. . . ."

Stony shrugged and eased back a step. "Up to you, Pop. If you ain't interested, that's your right, and you can just ride on out, no hard feelings."

Pop warily scanned the other outlaws, arrayed in front of the rock house. Everybody seemed mighty casual, but Pop's self-preservation instinct was screaming at the top of its lungs. He hadn't survived this long in the Devil's Kitchen by being trusting, which was to say stupid. He had a strong hunch that Stony would kill him rather than let him leave The Roost, for fear he might have some allegiance to Clyde, and warn the last of the Bohannons of Stony's scheme. Stony Brown's favorite motto was "better safe than sorry," and if it took putting Pop six feet under to be safe, Stony wouldn't blink one bulging eye.

"Okay," said Pop reluctantly, feeling trapped. "I'll do it."

"Mighty glad, Pop. Mighty goddamned glad. Give us ten minutes and we'll be ready to ride."

"Tonight?"

"Good gracious yes, hoss. The sooner we put Sam Slater under, the better we'll all feel. Ain't none of us gonna get a wink of sleep anyhow, knowing he's prowling around in the Devil's Kitchen, the son of a bitch."

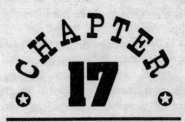

CHAPTER 17

IN SPITE OF THE FACT THAT HE DIDN'T WANT Rachel Myers to get too big a head start, Slater had taken the time to go back to the canelo and retrieve his canteen, Spencer carbine, and the gunnysack of money purloined from the Farmers & Merchants Bank by Black Jack and his gang.

The carbine was still in its scabbard, beneath the dead horse. Slater uncinched the saddle and used Bryner's cowpony to drag the hull out from under the carcass. He tied his own rope pommel to pommel and worked the horse as though they were trying to keep a steer stretched out for branding.

Untying the scabbard from his saddle, he transferred it to Bryner's rimfire, hanging it on the apple. Bryner's repeater rode in a boot cinched on the offside. Figuring two rifles were enough, he discarded Clyde's long gun and proceeded after Rachel.

Though he often had to make his own loads for the Spencer—the .56 caliber, copper-cased bottle-necks were becoming increasingly hard to find—Slater was partial to the carbine. The Spencer had come into its own during the Civil War, giving Union forces a crucial firepower advantage. Rueful Confederates said of the Spencer that a man could load it on Sunday and shoot all week. Its eight round capacity, seven in the tubular magazine and one in the chamber, had been something to talk about back in those days.

Now, though, there were quite a few repeating rifles with greater capacities. The Henry carried sixteen rounds fully loaded, and the Winchester rifle carried fifteen. Still, Slater stuck to the Spencer. Not once had it failed him, and he had seldom needed more than eight rounds to get the job done.

After a few miles on Miss Bounty's trail, he concluded that she wasn't going to make good enough time to get clear of the Devil's Kitchen before tomorrow, not while towing a horse and two ornery mules draped with the bodies of Black Jack and the Lukan brothers. This being the case, he further concluded that she would hole up somewhere come full night. The Kitchen was not the kind of country you risked traveling in the dark unless you knew the way. Besides, there was a new moon, and the next few nights were going to be mighty dark indeed.

With this in mind, Slater paced his horse.

Bryner's cayuse was a roan cowpony, strong and agile, but it hadn't had much rest, or any graining, for several days. The canelo could live off snake-weed for a month and still run like the wind from can-see to can't-see, but Slater doubted that Bryner's roan was fit for a long, hard gallop over rough terrain.

Several times during the scorching heat of the afternoon, he dismounted and walked the horse for a spell. Twice he gave it a little water, poured into the crown of his hat. He took none himself. He knew of no trustworthy springs between his present location and the Sunset Rim. None, anyway, that could be reached without a time-consuming detour from his present course.

He figured Rachel didn't know of any either. Far as he knew, she had never worked in this area. He had heard of her mostly out Texas way, or up in the Indian Territory—prime outlaw country in its own right—and he had run across her that one time on the Bloody Border, when both of them had been after Johnny Madrid. The Devil's Kitchen was bad medicine if you didn't know its secrets, or didn't travel with someone who did.

For a while, Whitmore's sign paralleled Rachel's, and at first Slater thought the Hanksville man was also after Rachel. But when the canyon emptied into a high sagebrush valley from which several other barrancas radiated, like spokes on a wheel, Whitmore's sign veered one way while Rachel's went another. Apparently he was no longer interested in anything but escape. Slater resolved to deal with him after he'd collected the reward on Bohannon. The reward, rightfully his, that Rachel Myers was doing her best to steal.

He spent much of the afternoon trying to decide what he would do to her by way of repayment for her treachery. He tried to persuade himself that he should deal with her without regard to her gender. She was every bit as dangerous as a man. *More* dangerous, in fact, precisely because she was a woman, and hence the recipient of special consideration. No matter how cold-blooded, most men second-thought violence toward a woman. The hesitation might be fleeting, measurable only in fractions of a second, but Rachel Myers was the type to make a man sorry for it.

You better learn your lesson, Slater warned himself. *Just remember, she left you back there to die. Next time, if it comes down to it, she'll pull the trigger herself.*

As a blood-red sunset painted the western sky, he saw the swarm of buzzards congregating a mile or so up ahead, and urged the roan into a more lively gait. In short order he made a discovery that proved Rachel Myers had made a serious and costly mistake.

The spring looked inviting, especially after a scorcher like today. Cool water trickled out of horizontal cracks in a jutting ledge, weeping down the stone to drip into a crescent-shaped pool beneath the ledge. A dozen buzzards circled low in the sky, and as many more fed on the bloated carcasses of two mules and a horse. The last time Slater had seen that horse, it had been carrying Black Jack's body.

The spring was poison. More than a few in the Devil's Kitchen were like that. Nobody knew why it happened, what element made the water bad, but it was something neither man nor animal could discern before it was too late to do anything but die.

The sign told the story. Rachel had let the mules and horse drink while she dismounted to loosen her own mount's cinch. Apparently one of the now-dead animals had displayed symptoms that warned her in time to keep her own horse away from the pool.

Loading Bohannon's carcass aboard the last remaining horse, she had walked away. Slater estimated that only a few hours separated them now. He was absolutely sure he could catch her.

The Lukan brothers were still lashed to the dead mules, and the buzzards were not bothering to make distinctions between mule and human flesh. It was a grisly sight, but it didn't bother Slater. The business he was in was not for the squeamish or faint of heart. He had seen worse.

He decided to leave the Lukans. He couldn't spare the time to bury them, and he didn't have the means to take them along. There would be no point in coming back later to collect them. In a day or two the bones of dead men and animals would be picked clean.

Riding on, he predicted that come morning a

great many more buzzards would be on hand to partake of this scavenger's feast. They would be visible in the sky for many miles. Slater assumed that the Hanksville posse no longer posed a threat, but Clyde Bohannon was behind him, and the buzzards would point the way for him.

Slater put several more miles behind him before full dark, made a cold camp under a bunch of scrub cedar, and was on the trail again long before sunrise.

An hour later he came upon the dead horse. Rachel Myers was nearby, lying facedown. The horse had been shot through the head. Drawing his short gun, he stopped the roan and aimed the Schofield at Miss Bounty.

"Stand up," he said.

She didn't move.

"Get up or you're going to be dead for real."

He thumbed the hammer back.

"Damn it!" she swore.

She rolled over and sat up. The .32 Savage was in her hand. She didn't make the mistake of pointing it at Slater.

"Nothing goes right anymore," she complained, and skewered him with an angry glower. "How did you know?"

"Simple. The horse has been dead since sometime early last night. You can see that plain enough just looking at it. Besides, I didn't hear a gunshot, and I was near enough I would have, had it happened this morning."

"That explains the horse. But how did you know I was playing possum?"

"Tracks. You ran yonder to that drywash. Then you walked back and lay down. Mighty active for a dead person. I figure you took cover when your horse went down. And when you saw me coming you decided to try an old trick."

"You don't miss much, do you?" she asked, disgusted.

"Try not to."

"They took Bohannon."

"I see that." Slater shook his head. "He's more trouble dead than he was alive. Who has him now?"

"All I know is the bastard made a long shot from that cedar ridge over there. Like you said, it was last night. I was heading that way to camp for the night. It was pitch dark, and I had just decided to settle in and wait for morning. Then the shot, and the horse went down. I don't know if he was aiming for the horse or for me and just missed. I didn't stop to ask. Ran back to the wash and kept my head down. This little .32 is as worthless as a four-card flush against a long gun."

Slater judged that the wash was scarcely fifty yards away.

"You didn't see him when he took Bohannon's body?"

"I said it was pitch black," snapped Rachel crossly. "I didn't see anything, or hear anything either."

Slater held the roan to a walk as he circled the

scene, reading sign. Returning to Rachel, he said, "One man."

"Well, there could have been more up on the ridge," she said in her own defense. Standing now, brushing dust off her clothes, she quirked a smile. "I could have shot you just now."

"You could have tried."

"You know, Slater, I just can't help but like you."

"Is that why you lit out on me yesterday?"

"I knew you could handle those bushwhackers. I wasn't worried."

"You weren't worried because you thought they'd shoot a whole week's worth of daylight through me."

"Sam, how could you think so poorly of me, after all we've meant to each other!"

Slater smiled faintly. He couldn't quite tell if she was being facetious or if she was really trying to sell him a bill of goods—not that it mattered.

"I just don't trust anybody."

"Yes, I know. Don't say it. Nothing personal."

"Right."

She shrugged. "All we can do is put the past behind us and deal with the present. We must get Bohannon back. Do you think that horse can carry double?"

"No."

"Looks game to me."

"I'm not saying it *couldn't*."

"You're saying you're going to leave me out here alone, without a horse?"

"I'm not worried."

"You sorry son of a bitch."

"Rachel! After all we've meant to each other, how could you talk to me that way?"

"Go to hell."

He touched the brim of his hat, mocking her.

"On my way, ma'am."

"I'll shoot you in the back if I have to, Slater!" she yelled as he reined the horse around.

"I don't think so," he replied, and rode away, holding the roan to a walk. Not once did he look back.

The man, thought Rachel, *is insufferably sure of himself.* She glanced at the .32 Savage, wondering if he'd just been gambling, or if somehow he had actually known the pistol was empty. Whoever had taken Black Jack off the dead horse had also taken the rifle out of the saddle scabbard. So now she was not only on foot in the middle of outlaw country, but also out of ammunition.

Watching Slater and his horse melt into the heat shimmer rising from the sun-hammered flats, Rachel Myers smiled.

"You think you've seen the last of me? Better think again, Sam Slater."

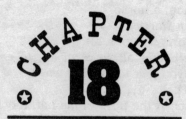

CHAPTER 18

SHAD MOWRY PICKED HIGH GROUND FOR night camp, on the windy rim of a sandstone butte. Chimneys and spires decorated the steep front face of the butte, and deeply eroded gullies cross-hatched the back slope. Palo verde grew in the washes, ironwood and blackbrush on the slope. Mowry hobbled the horses down-slope from camp, where they grazed on bunchgrass and Apache plume.

Digging a shallow hole in dirt trapped by run-off between two humps of slab rock, he built a small fire in the hole, using curl leaf to minimize the smoke. He figured the people he had to worry about would be traveling by way of the canyons and flats, and so wouldn't see his fire from below.

Beans and blackstrap simmered in a small skillet. Squatting beside the outlaw oven, he heard the water in the coffepot begin to hiss; the lid of the pot started to tap. He dug into a sack of Sultano with his free hand and threw some java into the pot. That done, he glanced across at Mattie, and realized it wasn't just Sam Slater and Clyde Bohannon he had to worry about.

Mattie had Black Jack's corpse propped up in a sitting position against a boulder. Bohannon's dead eyes seemed to bore right through Mowry. A crazy, crooked grin was frozen on his chalk-white face. Mowry could smell that sweet-sour stench of decaying flesh. The smell didn't cost him his appetite, but watching Mattie just about did the trick. She was kneeling beside the corpse, running a hand gently through Bohannon's matted hair. A cold shudder went through Mowry.

"What the hell are you doing?" he snapped.

"Just trying to make him look presentable."

"For what? You aim to take him to church come Sunday?"

"When we take him in I want him to look as good as he can. Black Jack Bohannon was a famous man."

"Famous?" Mowry snorted. "Look where it got him."

"He's got to look good," she insisted.

"He ain't gonna look nothing but dead from now on, no matter what you do. And *we* are not taking

him in. You are. I ride into Hanksville, they'll have
me playing host to a necktie party."

"You can trust me."

"At least close his eyes," said Mowry, disgusted.

He doubted he could trust her at all. Mattie
Ogham was as crazy as a horse with a bellyful of lo-
coweed. He knew that now; he only wished he'd
known it sooner, but he'd allowed his desire for her
to blind him.

Ever since they'd taken Bohannon's corpse
away from that woman bounty hunter, Mattie had
been carrying on like a person who was a few bricks
short a load. Mattie and the corpse had doubled up
on one of the horses, and all through the afternoon
Mowry had listened to her talking to Black Jack. It
beat all he'd ever seen, and he'd seen the elephant.
Talking to a damned corpse! She had berated the
dead man for up and dying on her before fulfilling
his promises to her, as though Bohannon had
kicked the bucket of his own free will! Then she'd
switch to murmuring sweet nothings, telling Black
Jack she was sure he understood why she was collecting the reward. Someone was going to, and of
course Jack would want it to be her.

Mowry shook his head as he poured steaming
portions of beans and blackstrap onto two tin
plates. A dash of cold water poured from canteen
into coffeepot settled the grounds, and he helped
himself to a cup of crank. A lot of outlaws didn't
mind a stale corn dodger and a snort of nose paint
for a trail supper, but Mowry preferred a hot meal,

and he seldom permitted circumstances to deny him that small pleasure.

"Here's some grub," he said, leaving her plate on the ground. Yesterday he might have taken it to her. Today he wasn't sure he wanted to get anywhere near her. And he was half afraid she'd say something about giving Black Jack a helping, in which case he was going to shoot her like the mad dog she was.

Mattie came over and sat down by the fire to eat, which surprised Mowry.

"Good," she mumbled through a mouthful. "Just think, Shad. Before long we'll be eating steaks and drinking champagne in some fancy restaurant, where the waiters all wear jackets as white as new snow, and the glasses chime like church bells when we drink a toast."

Mowry made no reply. A toast to good ol' Black Jack Bohannon, no doubt. He'd already made up his mind that he and Mattie Ogham were going to part company right quick and for good after he had his hands on the bounty. No point in telling her that.

"I been meaning to ask," said Mattie, smiling sweetly. "How much is the reward on you, Shad?"

A spoonful of supper frozen halfway between plate and mouth, Mowry stared at her. It suddenly came very clear to him what she was up to, and what the future held in store, and he was both angry and afraid at the same time.

"Oh, I get it," he said curtly. "Now I see." He dropped the spoon on the plate and the plate on the ground. Rising, he went to the rim of the butte and looked down into the night-filled canyon. He listened very hard. If she came sneaking up behind him he would grab her and throw her off. Yes, by God, that's what he would do. The same as she planned for him. As for collecting the reward, he would just have to find some other way.

He waited a couple of minutes, but she didn't make a move, so he spun on his heel and stalked back to the outlaw oven, stood over her with a hand resting on the butt of his Remington Army. She was calmly finishing her meal, and looked innocently up at him, as though there was nothing on earth wrong. Her attitude just made him angrier.

"That's the way it would be, isn't it?" he asked, his tone brusque and accusatory. "You'll stick with me until I'm worth a few thousand dollars laid out on a board. Then what? You go and find somebody to kill me, right? A new partner. And when he's worth killing, you'll play the same game all over again. That's how you got it figured. I'm not stupid, you know."

She stared at him a moment, then resumed eating, as though she hadn't heard a word he had said, or as if she had decided he was merely a raving lunatic that she was better off ignoring.

Furious, he reached down and grabbed her roughly, hauling her to her feet so violently that she lost her grip on the plate. It fell, clattering on the rocky ground. She whimpered as he shook her hard enough to rattle teeth.

"You crazy bitch!" he hissed. "What did I ever see in you?" He slapped her viciously. "You're nothing but a lousy whore."

In the darkness he did not see her blue eyes turn smoky gray, but he sure enough felt her wrath, even if he wasn't warned of its coming. Her knee rose sharply into his groin. Wheezing like a windbroke nag, Mowry doubled over, groping his private parts, a cold wave of nausea sweeping through him.

Mattie spun out of his grasp. Through a whirlwind of sick agony he realized she was going to try for the Winchester "Yellow Boy" leaning against his saddle. He stumbled desperately after her, tackling her. She kicked and clawed and howled like a trapped wildcat.

Rage overcoming pain, Mowry began hitting her with his fists. He struck her several times in the face. Half-conscious, mewling through a mouthful of blood, Mattie rolled over. Sucking air into his lungs, on hands and knees, he took a moment to recover. Head lolling, he glanced sideways at her. Her body was wracked by quiet sobbing; she was crying without making a sound.

"Mattie. . . ." he groaned, pinched by remorse.

"All I . . . all I wanted . . . was a purty dress."

He reached out to lay a hand on her trembling shoulder. She struck it away.

"Don't touch me, you bastard!"

Fresh anger swept like wildfire through him. He pounced on her, ripping savagely at her dress, snarling like the animal he had become. She screamed hoarsely, flailing at him. He scarcely felt the blows. He tore the dress off her body in pieces. Her skin was silver in the starlight. She screamed some more, and way off a coyote howled, perhaps in answer, and he hit her until the screaming died, until she was unconscious. Then he had his way with her, rough and quick.

Passion spent, he rolled weakly off her and lay looking for quite a long time at the star-glutted sky. That was all he had ever wanted from Mattie Ogham anyway, he told himself. He told himself that very thing, over and over again, but he couldn't shed a shadow of guilt, no matter how many times he told himself. Thoroughly disgusted with himself, he sat up to find Black Jack still staring at him.

"What are you grinning at, you son of a bitch?"

Black Jack didn't answer.

Mowry stood and buttoned his fly. "What about that, Jack?" he badgered, knowing he was a fool, or worse, for talking to a corpse, but compelled to do so just the same by the envy he still felt toward Bohannon. "What about what I done to your girl? Figured she was your own private property, didn't you? Just 'cause you said it was so. You always thought things had to be a certain way just 'cause you said. Well, it appears you were wrong, don't it? So what do you aim to do about it, you dumb bastard?"

Black Jack just grinned at him.

Mowry walked over, got a handful of Bohannon's shirt, caked with dried, black blood, and dragged the corpse toward the rim.

"I'm getting sick and tired of you grinning at me," muttered Mowry. "I didn't think it possible, but you smell worse now than you did when you were above snakes."

He laid the corpse on the brink and straightened the kink out of his spine, feeling faintly sick to his stomach.

"I'm gonna show you what I think of your sorry hide, Black Jack Bohannon. I'm going to kick you off this mountain. You ain't worth $2,000. You ain't worth squat, you damned . . ."

He heard her a second too late, and she hit him squarely in the back before he could spin to face her. Only then did she cut loose with a mad shriek. For one gut-twisting instant, Mowry tottered on the verge of the butte's sheer face. Twisting, he lashed out in frantic desperation, and then he was falling. Panic squeezed a guttural scream out of him. He didn't realize he had a handful of Mattie Ogham's cornsilk hair, or that Mattie was falling with him. All he knew was the fall itself—that indescribable, terrifying sensation—and a quick, excruciating burst of anger.

And then he knew nothing at all.

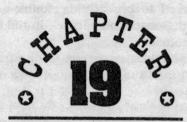

CHAPTER 19

SLATER WORKED HIS WAY UP THE SLOPE OF the butte as dawn light pearled the eastern sky. He made no more sound than the dawn as he climbed, Spencer in hand. Pausing in a clump of serviceberry, he scanned the camp. Twenty feet away stood two hobbled horses. Even this close, the horses did not hear or sense him, so silent—so Apache—was his approach.

He saw Black Jack Bohannon, stretched out near the rim. Flies were buzzing around Jack, and around scattered tinware near an outlaw oven. Two saddles, a rifle, blankets, all present and accounted for. Now where the hell was everybody?

Trailing these two horses from the spot where Rachel had been ambushed, he hadn't been able to tell if he was after one person or two. One of the horses looked to be carrying double—one rider sharing with Bohannon's corpse—but Slater hadn't been able to tell for sure.

It was possible that the owner, or owners, of the camp had heard him coming, and were now laying in wait, guns ready. He doubted it, but he hadn't survived this long by underestimating the enemy. So he spent another quarter of an hour circling the camp, using the utmost stealth, braced for a sudden burst of gunfire. As long as he heard the shot he'd be well satisfied. It was the one you didn't hear that killed you.

The reconnoiter convinced him this was no ambush. He was puzzled, but also relieved. He'd had just about all the ambushes he could stomach for one job.

To decide was to act with Slater, and as the sun climbed above the rimrock, he walked boldly out into the open. He made note of the scuffed ground, and the tattered shreds of what appeared to have been a gingham dress. Going to the rim of the butte, he looked down into an array of chimneys and spires—Mother Nature at her most artistic. He spotted the body of a man down there, too far down to identify. Slater returned to the saddles and blankets, searching for clues.

In one saddlebag he found $2,000 in greenbacks, wrapped in a shirt. In another he found a Montgomery Ward catalogue. Pages advertising the latest in women's apparel were particularly dog-eared. Slater's memory was jarred.

Now I'll never get those purty dresses he promised me . . . .

Words spoken by Mattie Ogham, standing over Bohannon a few days ago.

A closer study of the ground yielded a partial footprint which he surmised had been made by a barefoot woman. Could it have been Mattie? If so, who was she riding with? The money seemed to indicate it was a member of the Bohannon gang. Four members of the gang were dead. That left Clyde and one other whose identity Slater did not know.

Slater returned to the rim. Was that Clyde Bohannon down there? Where was the girl? He walked along the rim, searching the rocks below, and finally saw her, her body wedged between a couple of spires, like a shred of meat lodged between the fangs of a wolf.

He was curious to know what had transpired here, and tried to put it together, but pieces of the puzzle were missing.

Wasting little time on guesswork, he wrapped Black Jack in a blanket and tied the bundle with rope. Saddling one of the horses, he put the body belly-down across the hull and used more rope to lash it firmly in place. Removing the hobbles from the other horse, he left it behind, leading the other down the backside of the butte to the place where his own mount was hidden.

He left the rim a few minutes too soon to see the

cloud of dust boiling up at the far reach of an adjacent barranca. And he was several miles distant when the bunch of hard-riding hombres reached the base of the butte.

Apache Joe's eagle eyes spotted Mowry's body among the sandstone sculptures. Sick with fear for Mattie, Pop Ogham clambered clumsily through the chimneys and boulders, calling his daughter's name. John Buck was the one to find her, and called the others in. Seeing her bloody, broken remains, Pop sat down hard and began to shake violently. He felt suddenly old and worthless and alone.

"Don't appear she's been shot," remarked Buck, looking her over with cold-blooded detachment.

"Shad Mowry, either," said Clyde, scanning the rim above.

"God, I need a drink," croaked Ogham.

The others looked at him with more curiosity than compassion. They did not empathize with the old rewrite man's loss and so were unequipped to share in his grief, had they even been so inclined.

"Wonder what happened?" queried Buck, speaking for everyone but Stony. "Who cares?" barked Brown, impatiently. "Let's ride."

Clyde didn't like unanswered questions.

"Why don't you and Joe go up to the top and have a look around?" he suggested.

"What for? We're lookin' for Slater, remember?"

"Slater may have done this."

Ogham stared blankly at Clyde. Stony tugged on his scraggly beard and nodded.

"Maybe. I'll have a look-see. C'mon, you heathen."

As Stony and Apache Joe made for their horses, Three Fingers and John Buck went to Mowry, intent on confiscating boots, guns, shells, and anything else of value. Like the buzzards who would come later, they were scavengers in their own right.

Clyde went to his horse, fished a bottle of whiskey from his saddlebags, and came back to find Pop standing over Mattie's body. Ogham was leaning heavily against the base of a rock spire, dry heaving. Clyde offered the bottle.

"Obliged," mumbled Ogham feebly, surprised by this thoughtful gesture.

"Sorry about your girl, Pop."

"She . . . she was all I had."

"Yeah."

Ogham sat down again, and had emptied the bottle by the time Stony Brown and Apache Joe returned from their scout.

"Camp up there on the rim," said Stony. "One horse, one saddle. And this."

He handed Ogham the Montgomery Ward catalogue. Most of the Devil's Kitchen outlaws knew about Mattie and her wishbook.

Pop took the catalogue and clutched it tightly to his chest. He cut a tragic, pitiable figure, but

Stony was unmoved, and dispassionately continued with his report.

"Saw sign of two horses going away from the camp, headed west. Fresh tracks, not more'n an hour or two old, I'd say."

"Moccasin tracks, too," grunted Apache Joe.

"Indians?" muttered Three Fingers, having finished with Mowry.

Apache Joe shrugged. "He moves like an Indian."

"Some say Slater's half Apache," offered Stony.

"Had to be Slater," said Clyde.

Ogham again stared blankly at him. "Slater killed my girl?"

"Could be, Pop."

"Looks like that ain't all he did to her," said Buck.

"Stow it, John," snapped Clyde.

"Wherever he is, he can't be too far ahead of us," said Stony. "The Sunset Rim's less than a half day's ride. I say we get there, pronto. We could get lucky and cut his trail."

Clyde nodded. Since leaving Swope's place yesterday morning, they had come across a horse and two mules dead at a poison spring, and followed the tracks of two riders from there, one traveling well ahead of the other. Farther on, yet another dead horse was come upon. From there, the trail of one rider had led them here. Was that rider Sam Slater? Clyde was inclined to think so. The Regulator left a trail of death and destruction wherever he went.

No man knew the Devil's Kitchen better than Clyde Bohannon, and he was quick to realize that from this butte there were only a few ways out through the Rim. He calculated that from the Rim they could see across the desert flats west of the Kitchen for fifty miles, maybe more. If Slater was heading for Hanksville, chances were fair to middlin' they'd spot him, or his dust.

"Okay," he said. "We're burning daylight."

The others were turning for their horses when Pop said, "We can't leave her like this."

"The hell we can't," said Stony.

"No," said Pop flatly. "Can't leave her to the buzzards and coyotes. Just can't, that's all."

Stony glowered, snorted, and took another step toward the mounts.

"Least we can do is pile rocks over her," conceded Clyde.

"Are you loco?" railed Stony. "While we're piling rocks, Slater's putting more miles between him and us."

"Go on, then," said Clyde calmly. "Pop and I will catch up."

Stony thought it over and looked at Three Fingers, Apache Joe, and John Buck, all the while tugging fiercely on his beard. There was no good reason that he could see not to take Bohannon's suggestion. If they got to Slater first they could take Black Jack's carcass and worry about Clyde later.

Making up his mind, Stony started toward the

horses for a third time. The other three followed. Clyde watched them ride away.

"How come you done that for me?" asked Pop.

Clyde said nothing, just stood there, watching.

Ogham drew a ragged breath. "I got to tell you, Clyde. You done right by me. Least I can do is the same by you. They were aimin' to ventilate you, Clyde, and collect the bounty on Black Jack for themselves."

Pop figured Clyde would get mad at him for not fessing up sooner. Instead, Bohannon smiled lazily.

"I'm not surprised. That would be just like Stony Brown, the two-faced, split-tongued, sawed-off, little runt."

"You mean . . . you mean you suspected all along?"

"Why do you think I pulled this little stunt? We'll let them tangle with Slater, then we'll move in and finish the job. That's the best way I can see to get my brother back."

"You didn't mean what you said? About piling rocks on Mattie so's the coyotes can't get to her?"

Clyde gave Pop a long, hard look.

"Might as well," he allowed. "No harm in letting Stony and his boys get a head start."

And so they laid Mattie out in a low place, and Pop gently put the wishbook on her belly and crossed her arms over it. They piled rocks, working up a sweat. When they were done, Pop stood over the grave with head bowed, and Clyde was taken aback, for he hadn't imagined that Pop and the Almighty were on speaking terms.

A moment later Ogham set his slouch hat on his head, pulling it down low over his eyes. He noticed the funny way Clyde was looking at him.

"I reckon Slater done it, like you said, Clyde. Before, I didn't see as how I had any stake in this. Now I do. I ain't no gunslinger like Johnny Buck, and I ain't crazy mean like Apache Joe or Three Fingers, but I know a few tricks. So if they don't kill Slater first, and if you don't, I reckon I'll have to do the job my own self."

Clyde had never heard Pop Ogham talk like this. He had always figured Ogham for a wily, old fox who preferred slinking away from trouble, rather than facing it square. But Pop had changed suddenly. Something hard and cold and resolute glimmered in his eyes.

"Yes," said Clyde, as Pop passed him on his way to the horses. "Yes, I reckon you will."

CHAPTER 20

SLATER WAS HAPPY TO PUT THE DEVIL'S Kitchen behind him. Now only twenty-odd miles of sagebrush and saguaro lay between him and collecting the reward at Hanksville. By morning he would be rid of Black Jack Bohannon's troublesome remains and $2,000 richer. He had all but about $4,000 of the money taken from the Farmers & Merchants Bank, of which he would return every red cent. Then a bath, a shave, a meal, and a bed. After that? Well, he still had a score to settle with one George Whitmore.

Black Jack Bohannon had been a load of double-certified trouble, but Slater had the feeling that was all behind him now. He had only himself to blame, anyway. Joining up with the posse had been his first mistake. That hadn't been his style; call it a moment of weakness. He was a loner who knew only too well the dark side of human nature, and every time he gave so-called decent, law-abiding folks the benefit of the doubt, he ended up being plenty sorry. George Whitmore's dark side was a match for Black Jack's, and this he should have known. Everytime he forgot, life came running up to smack him a good one, like a schoolmarm who had to take the rod to a recalcitrant student just to get him to learn his lessons.

Then there was the matter of Rachel Myers. Slater told himself he should have recognized her from the first, all the hymn-singing and Bible-thumping aside. Sheer carelessness on his part. If he kept making mistakes like that one, his career as a bounty hunter would soon come to a sudden and violent end.

It surprised him that he couldn't get Rachel out of his mind. He kept wondering if she would make it out of the Devil's Kitchen alive. Now, why did he care? She hadn't been too concerned about his health and well-being, leaving him behind in that canyon death-trap.

Putting the Sunset Rim behind him, he came to a stretch of sand dunes. Down in the hollows grew Indian rice grass, stirrup-high clumps that made good graze. The Indians made bread from its seed heads. The horses had a tough go in the shifting white sand, and much of the way Slater walked them. He figured he could put another five or six miles behind him before nighting out on the desert plains.

He was a mile out on the sagebrush flats when something smacked into the arm of a saguaro six feet to his right and came out the back in a spray of green cactus pulp. He knew what that something was, and the gunshot that followed a second later only verified it.

Somebody was shooting at him.

He checked the roan sharply and looked back.

Four riders, a good half mile away, and as he looked he saw another puff of powdersmoke. The slug chunked into the ground, too close for comfort. No ordinary rifle, and no ordinary shooter either, to get so close at this range. He couldn't tell who it was, and he wasn't going to linger just to find out.

The lead rope tied to the other horse's split-ear bridle was dallied around his saddlehorn, and Slater freed it before goading the roan into a standing-start gallop. He held the reins in one hand and the lead rope in the other. If you could help it, you didn't keep two horses tied together when you were making a run for it. If one went down the other did, too, and then you played hell.

He wished he still had the canelo. Bryner's cowpony didn't have much stamina left. The roan had been too long away from its T Anchor home ground, and all the finish had worn off.

No way he could outdistance them.

Nothing to do but turn and make a stand.

Whoever they were, they had to be outlaws. Rachel had said Clyde Bohannon would put the word out, and the Devil's Kitchen hardcases would hit the trail. By hook or crook, outlaws generally had the best mounts in the territory—racers and blooded stock. Their lives depended on fast horses. This was one race they were bound to win.

A dry wash loomed ahead. The roan stumbled on the steep bank. At the same moment, the horse carrying Bohannon screamed and went down, laying a furrow in the ground, shot dead in midstride. Concentrating too hard on staying aboard the roan, Slater let go of the lead rope a heartbeat too late. The rope went taut and yanked him sideways out of the saddle. He landed hard and rolled down the bank.

The roan veered down the wash, the path of least resistance, and came to a leg-spraddled halt a short distance away, head down and sides billowing, bit-worked foam drooling from its mouth. Slater got up and ran to it, pulling the Spencer and Bryner's repeater out of their respective boots. He retrieved the gunnysack as well. The bank's money was in it, and Hazen's Bible, with its cutout full of derringer, as well as a pouch filled with extra loads for the Spencer. In preparation for situations just like this one, Slater liked to have all the essentials together, ready for the quick grab.

A scatter of gunfire joined the thunder of hooves, and he wondered what they thought they were shooting at. He could stand up straight and not be seen; the wash was that deep. Conserving ammunition was a habit inculcated in him by Apache teachers.

The wash ran roughly north-south through the flat, and now Slater spun and jogged north, back to the spot where he had entered it so gracelessly. Stashing the repeater there, he ran another twenty yards, dropped the gunnysack under a palo verde tree clinging sideways to the bank, then climbed to the rim.

The four riders were spread out and riding hard, a hundred yards away. They were looking and shooting at the spot where he had disappeared. By appearing elsewhere, he enjoyed a brief advantage, and made the utmost of it.

Bringing the carbine to shoulder, he fired twice, so swiftly that the reports blended into one crackling peal of gun thunder. Two horses fell. Two men went flying. The others veered off, returning fire. Slater stood rock-steady in a hail of hot lead. They were off guard and shooting wild, and he counted on luck for enough time to fire once more, sighting carefully. A third horse reared and toppled sideways, hurling its rider ten feet.

Slater jumped down into the wash and ran south. He didn't like killing horses, but he did what he had to. With one of his own horses dead and the other bottomed out, he was at a disadvantage unless he could put the enemy afoot, as well. With scant seconds in which to aim and fire, he'd picked the bigger targets.

The horse carrying Bohannon had fallen near

the rim, and now Slater crawled up the bank to it, using its bulk as a breastwork of sorts. Black Jack's body was still securely lashed to the saddle. He could cut the rope with his clasp knife easily enough, but a thousand pounds of dead cayuse was resting on Bohannon's head and upper torso.

He chanced a look over the dead horse. The last mounted outlaw had wisely stepped down. His horse trotted off, spooked by the blood smell from the other horses. The longrider started running for the wash, aiming for a point well south of Slater's position, clearly hoping to flank the bounty hunter.

Laying the Spencer across the withers of the dead horse, Slater squeezed off a shot. The outlaw sprawled, and for an instant Slater thought he had pulled off a damned fine shot, but then the man yelled something to his colleagues and commenced running again. Slater didn't get another chance at him. The other three owlhoots, belly-down out there somewhere in the sagebrush, put down a heavy cover fire. Bullets sang over Slater's head and thumped into the carcass of the horse.

Slater took stock of the situation. The three in front of him were bound to be crawling closer, while the fourth man worked around behind him. He had to deal with the flanker first.

Crawling back to the wash, he slipped over the rim on his belly and rolled down the embankment. The roan still stood a few yards away. Slater looked beyond the horse, south, down the wash. That was the direction from which the flanker would come, either straight up the wash or along the rim. Slater decided to meet him halfway and get it over with.

As he passed the roan he grabbed hold of a bridle cheekstrap. The horse balked, disinclined to move another inch. Slater gave the bridle a curt tug and murmured a little Apache horse talk. The cowpony wearily surrendered to the inevitable and fell into step.

Walking with the horse's head over his right shoulder, the Spencer in his left hand, Slater paid special attention to the west rim of the dry wash. The sun was a ball of red fire low in the western sky, and Slater figured a smart hombre would put his back to it. In doing so he would also force Slater to look directly into the sun, a real liability in a gun duel.

This was precisely what John Buck did, appearing so suddenly on the rim that the roan snorted and shied sideways. The gun in the Texas-born shootist's hand jumped and spit flame. The impact of the bullet spun Slater around. The roan reared, pulling him off balance. This saved his life, for Buck was shooting again, and the bullet narrowly missed its mark. Slater fell to his knees, letting go of the horse. His left arm was numb. He dropped the Spencer, drew the Schofield, and fired.

His bullet struck the gunslinger high in the leg. Buck lost his balance and tumbled down the bank. Slater waited until he reached bottom before shooting again. Buck slammed back against the slope. A blossom of scarlet appeared on his shirt front. He sat down hard, spat a mangled cheroot out of his mouth, and looked with curious wonder across the wash at Slater, like he couldn't believe Slater had actually beaten him. Slowly, painfully, he lifted his gun. Slater fired a third time. This one died hard, so he put the third bullet between the eyes.

Checking his injury, he found that Buck's bullet had gouged a deep groove across the underside of his left arm, just below the elbow. Tearing away the sleeve, he laid the hot barrel of the Schofield against the wound, slowing the profuse flow of blood.

One down, three to go. If he didn't do better from here on there wouldn't be enough left of him in one piece to bury.

Somehow he had to get the other three in close and bunched together.

Staring across the wash at John Buck's mortal remains, he suddenly knew just how to accomplish that.

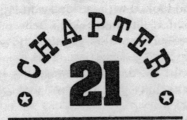

CHAPTER 21

"LOOK THERE!" CROWED STONY BROWN. "IT'S John Buck!" He stood up and threw his hat in the air. "By God, that tall, Texas son-of-a-bitch has done for Sam Slater!"

Apache Joe and Three Fingers Smith stood up, too. The dry wash was about a hundred yards distant, and there on the rim stood Buck, motioning for them to come on before disappearing down into the cut once more.

Stony let loose a war whoop of pure jubilation. He grinned at the old Indian outcast and the bear-sized mountain man.

"Let's go collect our dear departed friend, Black Jack Bohannon."

They bent their steps toward the wash, converging on the dead horse with the bundle-wrapped body tied across. Apache Joe drew his Bowie knife from its boot sheath and cut the rope binding Bohannon's corpse to the saddle. Three Fingers stepped in and grabbed saddlehorn and cantle. Grunting with exertion, he lifted saddle, horse, and all, enough so that Stony and Apache Joe could pull Black Jack clear.

Stony stood over the body a moment, savoring sweet success, immense satisfaction lighting up his face. This had turned out to be a heap easier than he had even dared imagine. Sam Slater hadn't been such a tough nut after all.

"Y'know, boys," he said, "I got to admit I always kinda envied ol' Black Jack here. Yessir, it seemed to me like the whole territory was forever talkin' about him. People always sayin' what a big bad hombre he was. How he was the worst outlaw ever drew breath, next to Jesse James." Stony snorted. "He sure don't look so big and bad now, does he? I'm right glad all those good, decent folk think so highly of him that they're willin' to pay $2,000 for the privilege of plantin' his bones in their grave pasture."

"He sure stinks," rumbled Three Fingers, making a face. "Smells worse'n a damned redskin."

Apache Joe looked askance at that comment. Three Fingers glowered back. He hated all Indians, Joe included. Only reason he hadn't taken Joe's scalp was he hadn't quite figured out yet how to do it without losing his own hairpiece.

Stony laughed. "Ya'll go on ahead and butcher each other. Be my guests. Means I'll only have to split the reward with Johnny Buck. Hell, he's earned his share."

Apache Joe leaped agilely to the bottom of the wash. Buck was strolling in from the south. His hat was pulled low, and his left arm hung stiffly, the sleeve torn and bloody. So the Texas gun artist hadn't got out of it unscathed. Apache Joe figured no man could have, against a two-legged lobo wolf like Sam Slater.

"Hey, Joe!" Stony was standing on the edge of the embankment, pointing north. "Go fetch that gunnysack yonder. I got a hunch we'll be wantin' what's in it."

Apache Joe turned his back on John Buck and made for the gunnysack lying beneath a palo verde tree clinging tenaciously to the bank.

Suddenly Stony was shouting an alarm, his "Make smoke, boys!" punctuated by the booming reports of handguns at close quarters, a shocking sound no matter how often a man heard it. Apache Joe whirled to see Stony and Three Fingers falling. The mountain man pitched forward off the bank. The ground trembled as he struck the bottom and lay still. Guns in both hands, John Buck was shooting—but it wasn't Buck. Now Apache Joe could see that, and he hated Sam Slater for tricking them, even as he felt grudging admiration.

Slater had employed an old Apache trick. How many times had broncos on the warpath ambushed a scouting party, then donned the uniforms of the dead horse soldiers, with the intent of riding into the yellowleg camp and wreaking further havoc? Slater had put on Buck's black vest, trousers, boots and hat, and lured them neatly in for close killing.

Apache Joe swept his sawed-off shotgun into line and fired full choke. His favorite load was pot-luck—a mix of buckshot, shoeing nails and small, sharp pebbles. At close range it could turn a man into raw meat.

But Slater was a shade faster than Apache Joe. Lunging sideways, he rolled and came up shooting. Apache Joe's mixed loads shredded nothing but thin air. Slater, however, didn't miss. Joe staggered backward, dropping the empty scattergun. Somehow he managed to stay on his feet, swaying precariously. He couldn't tell where he had been hit, but he knew he was hit bad.

As Slater closed in, Apache Joe groped for his sidegun. The bounty hunter struck it from his grasp. Apache Joe fell and tried to get up, reaching for the Bowie knife in his boot. Slater kicked the Kansas neck-blister out of his hand. Flat on his back, Apache Joe looked up into the barrel of Slater's Schofield, then past it to a pair of blue eyes as cold as winter ice.

"Go ahead," taunted Apache Joe, strangling on his own blood.

He was unarmed and defenseless, but that didn't deter Slater. Apache Joe had murdered many defenseless people in his time, without hesitation or remorse. He was a mad-dog killer, and Slater figured he'd be saving a few lives by ending this one. A good trade, in his book. Some would say this act made him as bad as Apache Joe, but they could say what they wanted. Thanks to Slater, they would sleep easier at night.

"Glad to oblige," he said, and pulled the trigger.

With a roar like a wounded grizzly's, Three Fingers charged. Slater whirled and fired. The hammers of both guns, his and John Buck's, fell on empty chambers. He dropped and rolled into the mountain man's legs. Three Fingers struck the ground and bounced right back up. *Mighty spry,* mused Slater, *for a man with two slugs in him.*

The bounty hunter dived for the repeater leaning against the bank—Bryner's long gun. Three Fingers caught him first, spinning him around, driving a fist as big and hard as a cannonball into Slater's face. Slater landed on his back some distance away, looking up into a darkening sky filled with peculiar swirling lights, feeling the earth tremble beneath him, his mouth and sinus passages filling with warm salty blood.

He managed to get to his hands and knees in time to take a kick in the gut. Rolling, awash with incredible pain, sucking for air, Slater counted himself lucky that the kick hadn't caught him higher or lower. Higher and he'd have a mess of bone splinters instead of a ribcage. Lower and his private parts would have been bloody pulp. He had to be thankful for small favors.

Trying to stand, he discovered that he couldn't make everything work in unison; he had to concentrate on each arm and each leg individually, a process entirely too time-consuming. Still snarling like a wild animal, Three Fingers grabbed him and lifted him clean off the ground. Slater punched him in the throat. The snarl became a screech. Smith dropped him, stumbling backward.

Slater pressed his advantage, moving in, focusing on the bloodied front of the mountain man's buckskin shirt. Three Fingers had taken two bullets in the chest. Slater slipped in and hammered a fist into his sternum. A torrent of blood spewed out of Smith's gaping mouth. He staggered but refused to fall. Slater circled warily, crouched, none too steady himself.

Three Fingers turned with him, eyes mad with rage and pain, blood matting the beard that covered his face. He swung massive arms to fend off Slater's feints. He wasn't thinking anymore, just reacting. And remembering. A dim recollection from a dim past, of a winter's-end struggle between bear and wolf, when the first thaw and ravenous hunger brought these creatures to steep mountain slopes, where they searched for dead animals long buried under now-melting snow, and where they sometimes fought each other for prime feeding ground. He was the bear, Slater the wolf. Overpowering strength pitted against quickness and cunning.

Slater wasn't feeling too quick. What was it going to take to put this buckskin-clad giant down for good? For the first time in a long time he felt exhaustion overtake him, slowing him. Several times Smith grazed him with those massive, flailing fists. Even half-killed, Three Fingers was his match hand-to-hand.

This conclusion turned him away, abruptly sprinting across the sandy bottom of the dry wash for Bryner's repeating rifle. Three Fingers lumbered after him, hot on his heels. Slater lunged the last few feet, grabbed the rifle, and rolled to put his back against the embankment. He worked the lever action—he couldn't count on there being a shell in the breech. There was. The ejected spell went spinning away, replaced by another. Three Fingers leaped. His bulk blotted out the sky. Slater fired point-blank. Smith sagged, his belly braced against rifle, the rifle in turn braced against the bank upon which Slater lay.

The bounty hunter levered, fired, levered, fired. Hot lead ripped through the mountain man, tearing huge holes in his back, spraying blood and flesh fragments across the wash. Three Fingers pounded Slater with his fists. By degrees the blows weakened, the light of life in his eyes gradually sputtered and went out. He fell sideways off the rifle, twitched, and was still forever.

Slater closed his eyes and for some time lay there against the embankment. Next he knew, night had fallen. Sheer willpower got him to his feet. He had no strength left. Despite what some people said,

he was human. He had to have rest. Dragging the
rifle, he stumbled like a drunk twenty yards north,
up the wash, before lying down, falling down, really,
to sleep.

CHAPTER 22

SLATER WOKE IN A HURRY WHEN THE BUZ-zard landed on his back. He rolled over and tried to hit the scavenger with the rifle as it took wing, but missed.

Daylight greeted him, and he was surprised that he had slept through the night. He was sore from head to toe; Three Fingers had delivered a few good licks. His arm hurt like hell, but he no longer felt the weight of utter exhaustion.

A great many buzzards circled overhead. More than a few were feeding on the corpses farther down the wash. *This has been a good week for buzzards,* thought Slater. Some watched with wary insolence as he walked near. He didn't intend bothering them. They served a purpose—they kept the desert clean.

Their purpose was not unlike his own—he collected society's garbage.

Speaking of which . . . he climbed the east bank of the dry wash and found several buzzards perched on Black Jack's remains. The blanket tied around the corpse was an obstacle to them, and they were trying to pick holes in the thickly woven wool. Slater hazed them away. One flew, the rest hopped to the dead horse, joining others of their kind already hard at work.

It occurred to Slater that just about everybody and everything wanted a piece of Black Jack Bohannon.

He searched in vain for the roan, finally concluding that Bryner's cowpony had made tracks for home ground. The T Anchor spread was south of Hanksville, and not too far from here. Like most other animals, horses had a well-developed homing instinct. The roan was long gone.

The one outlaw horse left alive stood a few hundred yards away. Slater didn't even try to guess why it hadn't headed back for the Devil's Kitchen. He could see the Sunset Rim to the east, a blue line of high ground on the horizon.

Hoping to catch the horse, Slater struck out across the flats. No such luck. The horse loped away as he drew near. He tried to Indian-up on it the next time, but to no avail. The horse would let him get only so close before running.

This merry chase, a classic exercise in futility, took Slater a half mile from the dry wash before he gave up. It was impossible to tell what a horse might do, or what mood it was in on any given day. As a rule, horses were dumb, fractious, unpredictable beasts, with few exceptions, one of the most notable being the canelo, which Slater started missing all over again.

Returning to the wash, he had second thoughts about killing the outlaw horses. Under the circumstances, though, it had been the correct decision, even if it did make getting to Hanksville look tough this morning.

He paused at each dead horse in turn. In two cases he was able to retrieve canteens. Cutting pieces of rope with Apache Joe's Bowie knife, he made a sling for both his Spencer and Bryner's repeater. He had a hunch he wasn't out of the woods just yet. Having studied plenty of wanted posters, he knew who these yahoos were. Perhaps more important for the future, he knew Clyde Bohannon wasn't among them.

Stony Brown, Apache Joe, Three Fingers Smith, and John Buck—altogether they were worth a great deal of reward money. Without at least one horse he couldn't haul them in. Best he could do was carry one on his back, which would make it a real long walk to Hanksville. But after all this he sure wasn't going to go back empty-handed; Black Jack was worth the most.

He had become rather fixated on the idea of taking Bohannon in. The harder the job, the more determined he became to see it through to the bitter end. Stubborn pride? Maybe, but a whole lot of people, most of them with their toes permanently curled now, had tried their utmost to keep him from finishing what he had set out to accomplish. If he had to take on the whole territory, he was going to finish what he had started, by God.

It was a shame, though, that he didn't have a wagon in his hip pocket, what with all these outlaws turning up dead. Could he collect on them all, he'd be sitting pretty, but there wasn't much chance of getting back in time to recover anything recognizable, and therefore collectible. The desert's scavengers would make short work of the corpses.

As a matter of personal taste, he shucked John Buck's clothes and retrieved his own, left in a pile next to the body of the Texas gunslinger. The desert moccasins Slater favored were doubly important now. They were much better suited to the task at hand than Buck's handtooled boots, with their underslung heels, narrow toe, and Lone Star cutouts.

With the rifles, canteens, gunbelt, and Schofield, not to mention Bohannon's body, Slater calculated all the weight he was proposing to carry fifteen-and-then-some miles to Hanksville. Worse the luck that Black Jack had been such a hefty pilgrim. So what about the gunnysack with the money, Hazen's special Bible, and the Spencer's extra loads? The latter he would certainly take. The rest he would bury here. No, he would be better off taking it all. He wouldn't let it be said that he had stashed the loot for himself.

Stuffing the cash into the blanket tied around Black Jack's body, he realized that another man in this situation would quite likely abscond with the money, and to hell with carting two hundred pounds of putrefied carcass fifteen miles. Eight thousand dollars in greenbacks was a damn sight lighter load.

But Slater couldn't bring himself to do it. He was unjustly wanted in Montana, where self-defense had been deemed cold-blooded murder. He didn't care to be wanted for anything else, justly or not. Too bad the Montana law couldn't see him now, and know his thoughts. Maybe then they'd realize how wrong they were about him.

The Bible under his shirt, canteens and rifles slung about his person, Slater hefted Bohannon onto one shoulder and put the morning sun, already a hellborn demon, at his back. Crossing the wash— no doubt the first of many such obstacles—he bent his steps westward. Laboring out of the deep cut, he concluded wryly that if the sun and the heat didn't kill him, the desert probably would.

He set an easy pace for himself. An Apache bronco could run all day without stopping. On occasion, during his years spent with Loco's Bedonkohe Chiricahua, he had done the same. Surely now, he could walk 'til sundown.

From the first he was tormented by thirst. He still had the copperish taste of blood in his mouth, but he saved the water sloshing in the two canteens for later in the day, when he knew he would really need it, and settled for rolling a pebble around in his mouth.

The sweltering miles passed slowly, and after a while he wasn't too sure they were passing at all. Every mile looked exactly like the previous one, and he began to wonder if he was making progress. Maybe he was dead—in hell. His mother had read him the Bible and Greek mythology when he was a boy. Now, suddenly, a memory shot across all the intervening years, from those fireside readings to this sun-scorched desert plain. He recalled the myth of Sisyphus, a Corinthian king condemned in Hades to roll a heavy stone up a steep incline. The stone always rolled back down to the bottom before he could take it to the top. Sisyphus was doomed to an eternity of fruitless, agonizing labor.

The flats were surrounded by mountain ranges, cobalt-blue teeth at the rim of the world, but the ones straight ahead, suspended in air above the heat shimmer, did not appear to be drawing one inch closer. *Maybe,* mused Slater, *I am dead, and condemned to an eternity of hauling Black Jack's stinking carcass across an endless wasteland.* Or maybe he was just delirious.

Bohannon was smelling awful ripe. That was real enough. Slater tried to ignore the stench of decaying flesh. In his present state, Black Jack made a skunk smell pretty. There was nothing Slater could do about it though, except persevere.

As the day wore on, Bohannon seemed to put on weight. Several hours from the wash, Slater calculated the bastard weighed about a half ton. He had to stop and roll the burden off his shoulder. He stood there, bent over, hands on knees. His legs trembled from terrible exertion. He expected to see the soles of his moccasins burst into flames. Seemed like he had to breathe two or three times just to get a breath of air. The sound of the water in the canteens tantalized him mercilessly; he refused to succumb.

He knew he could make it without Bohannon, no problem. But he simply could not bring himself to leave Black Jack behind.

Pressing on, he was forced to cross several deep, dry washes in quick succession. After that he began to stagger some. The flats gave way to rolling ground, where waves of blow sand made the going that much tougher. His aching leg muscles rebelled against the slightest incline. He sank to his ankles in hot sand, and taking a step became exquisite torture. The blazing sun seemed to stand still directly overhead, firmly fastened in a brass-colored sky, as though it refused to proceed further until he gave up and died.

How many miles had he put behind him? He had no way of knowing; time and distance were incalculable. His bloodshot eyes scanned the horizon, and it looked as it had from his starting point. Still he staggered on, impelled by sheer will, Apache steel, and stubborn pride. He muttered curses at Black Jack Bohannon, and at one point he thought he heard Bohannon chuckle.

Then he realized he was standing in a road, two dusty ruts grooved by the passage of many wheels over many years. He wasn't sure how long he'd been standing here. The ground vibrated underfoot. All he could hear was the rapid pounding of his strong heart. No, that wasn't all. The creak of timber, the rattle of trace chains, the drumroll of horses at road gait . . .

Looking right, he saw the stagecoach. It dipped down into a fold of earth, into the rippling, glassy surface of a mirage, disappearing. He did not dare believe in it until it reappeared, much closer now. He didn't even think about moving. The devil himself couldn't have budged him.

The stage driver climbed the leathers, hollering at the six-horse hitch to stop. The gun guard swung his sawed-off shotgun at Slater. The foam-flecked leaders, blowing hard, stopped scant feet from him.

"What in the blue blazes are you doin', standin' out in the middle of the road like that!" yelled the jehu, aggravated. "You tired of livin'?"

"Not anymore," said Slater.

CHAPTER 23

SLATER DIDN'T MUCH CARE FOR LOOKING UP into the twin barrels of the shotgunner's weapon, but he decided the man couldn't be blamed for his actions. The Devil's Kitchen outlaws had made life plenty interesting for folks hereabouts. Slater knew firsthand that the number of local longriders had been diminished by eight in the past week or so, but that didn't really count for much. Outlaws were like weeds in a garden patch. You could pull up a whole bunch, and next day there would be another bunch in place. One thing Slater never worried about was being out of work.

"Who the hell are you and where the hell did you come from?" snapped the gun guard, trying to scout around for signs of ambush and keep an eye on Slater at the same time.

Slater thumbed over his shoulder.

"The Devil's Kitchen?" asked the jehu, astonished.

"That's right."

"Where's your horse?"

"Do I look like I have a horse?"

"Fact is, you look like you walked plumb across the *malpais*."

"I did. Some of it."

"Well I'll be . . ." began the reinsman.

"You already are," said the gun guard crossly. "And a fool besides, if you believe him. This is a trick."

"You an outlaw, mister?" asked the driver bluntly.

"No," said Slater, thinking Montana would probably argue the point. "I'm a bounty hunter."

"What's that?" The jehu nodded at the blanket-wrapped bundle.

"Black Jack Bohannon, and some of the money he stole from the bank in Hanksville."

"Lord A'mighty!"

The gun guard finally lowered his ten-gauge. "You must be Sam Slater."

"Why do you say that?"

"Only man I know could've brought in a bravo mean as Black Jack Bohannon."

Flattery had little effect on Slater, particularly coming from a man who, only a moment before, had been a short prayer away from blowing a hole in him big enough to drive the stage through.

"Got room for me and Black Jack? I've done about all the walking I care to do for one day."

"Plenty," said the reinsman. "Only got one passenger. But as you can see, we ain't aimed at Hanksville, if that's where you're bound. Fact is, we left there this morning."

"What are you aimed at?"

"Fort Union mail run."

"Fort Union will have to do," said Slater. He wasn't so fixed on Hanksville that he would decline a chance to ride.

"We can put ol' Black Jack, damn his soul, up here on the top rack," offered the driver. "Won't charge you none, Mr. Slater. This here ride will be compliments of the stage company. We'll all breathe a lot easier knowing Bohannon is six feet under."

Slater nodded. "I'll need some help."

The gun guard laid his sawed-off aside and jumped down with a wiry agility that Slater envied. Together they handed Black Jack up to the jehu, a brawny man who had no trouble transferring the corpse onto the rail-encircled roof of the coach.

"Jesus," muttered the gun guard. "He's awful rank."

"Been dead awhile," said Slater.

"There'll be a handsome reward waitin' on you," said the driver.

"That's right as rain," seconded the shotgunner. "Four thousand simoleons."

"Four thousand? Thought it was two."

"Was. They tacked on another thousand for the robbery in Hanksville, and another after that when Bohannon killed the Moab sheriff."

"What are you talking about?"

"Sheriff Ashley. Black Jack done him in."

"When?"

"Few days ago, I reckon, up in the Devil's Kitchen. After the Hanksville robbery, Sheriff Elledge wired Moab, and Ashley led a posse in from there. Word is, the Bohannon gang bushwhacked 'em. Will Ashley was a fine man."

Slater stared at the shotgunner, trying to figure it out. He had been on Black Jack's trail, every foot of it, from the Sunset Rim to the side-canyon hideout where Bohannon had received his just desserts. There had been no sign of a bushwhack, or of a posse from Moab. Something wasn't right.

"Who said Bohannon killed Ashley?"

The two stageline employees looked at each other and shrugged in unison.

"Damned if we know," confessed the reinsman. "Word just got out, is all."

Slater shook his head. He was convinced the "word" was wrong. But he could see no profit in arguing the point with these two. If the authorities were determined to give him an extra thousand for a crime Bohannon could not have possibly committed, he wasn't going to complain, not after all the trouble he'd been through.

He was still pondering this mystery as he

walked back to the coach and opened the cambered door, so he wasn't as alert as he should have been. One foot on the iron step, he looked up at the gun a split-second before it went off.

The impact of the point-blank shot knocked him ten feet. He landed on his back, feeling like a bay steer had kicked him in the ribs. Blackness washed over him. When he could see again it was as though he was looking through heat shimmer. He could see Whitmore standing over him, but Whitmore was turning, swinging the gun away.

"Keep your hands off the scattergun," barked Whitmore as the gun guard reached for his weapon. The guard wisely became very still. The reinsman raised his hands.

"Both of you get down. Move!"

The stageline employees obeyed.

"Why the hell did you kill him?" asked the shotgunner, truculent.

"Hey, mister," said the reinsman, fearing for his life. "If this is a holdup, we ain't carryin' nothing' but the mail."

"Shut up!" rasped Whitmore, teetering on the brink of panic. He had to think. How could it have come to this? It wasn't just bad luck that had brought him and Slater together again; it was malicious fate. Why did God hate him? What had he ever done to deserve this?

He'd gotten out of the Devil's Kitchen alive, made it back to Hanksville, telling the people there that the Bohannon gang had shot up the posse, killing Ricker, separating him from the others. The word was out already about the ambushing of the Moab posse. As he had thought, the survivors of the ambush were blaming it on Bohannon.

But he had known it wouldn't last forever. Slater knew the truth about him. So did Bryner. With that in mind, he had packed a quick bag and caught this stage. He was making a run for it.

And then Slater had shown up.

He'd taken care of the bounty hunter—did it without thinking. He was too scared to think, too scared of what Slater might do to him. Now he had to keep killing.

The jehu read his own future in Whitmore's desperate eyes, and he didn't like what he saw.

"Now wait just a doggone minute," he said, his voice cracking. "You don't have to . . . I mean, whatever bad blood there was between you and that feller Slater, it ain't none of our business."

"Yes," said Whitmore, smiling crookedly. "Yes, it is your business. Sorry to say, you boys just happen to be in the wrong place at the wrong time."

He had always prided himself on his ability to think on his feet, to take any adversity and turn it to his advantage. Recently he had suffered more adversity all at once than he had known in a lifetime. So much, so quickly, that he hadn't been able to think it through. Now the panic left him. He was quite pleased with himself, with his inspiration. Even in this he could come out smelling like a rose.

Will Ashley's badge was still in his possession,

but not for long. Black Jack Bohannon's body lay on the top rack of the stagecoach. He had to make sure the badge was found on Bohannon. Then all he had to do was claim that the Bohannon gang had attacked the stage, killing Slater, the driver, and the gun guard. Only he had survived. And as he was the one to bring Black Jack's body in, he might even manage to get the reward. All he would have to worry about after that was Bryner, and he figured he could handle the T Anchor range rider. Surely he was smart enough to convince that ignorant cowboy to keep his mouth shut.

He thumbed back the hammer of his gun.

"I've got to do it, boys," he said, trying to sound like he was sorry. "No other way for me. Nothing personal. . . ."

"Sounds like something I'd say."

Whitmore whirled, heart leaping into his throat. He caught a brief, terrifying glimpse of Sam Slater, and then an even briefer glimpse of Slater's rock-hard fist, an instant before it smashed into his face. Whitmore next found himself lying on the ground, swallowing blood, his eyes watering. His nose was broken.

Slater hauled him upright and slammed him into the side of the coach. The gun guard pounced on the pistol Whitmore had dropped.

"Thought maybe you was gonna knock his block off," growled the shotgunner, obviously deploring Slater's failure to do so.

"I tried," said Slater.

"Let me," said the gun guard, vindictive. "I'll do better than try."

"Why was he goin' to shoot us?" wailed the reinsman. "What did we ever do to him?"

Slater was searching Whitmore for other weapons. He found none, but he did discover the badge.

"Lordamercy, that's . . . that looks like Will Ashley's tin star!"

"Beginning to make sense," said Slater, flipping the badge to the jehu.

"What are we gonna do with this coyote?" growled the guard.

Whitmore focused bleary eyes on Slater. "How? . . ." was all he could manage, strangling on his own blood.

Slater unbuttoned his powder-burned shirt and pulled out the Bible, now carrying one spent bullet in addition to the derringer.

"I reckon it's true the Lord looks out for fools," he said.

"I think I'm gonna start going to church come Sunday," murmured the driver.

"Save me a spot," said the gun guard. "First thing, I'll need to ask His forgiveness for what I'm about to do."

"Put the gun down," said Slater. "We're letting him go."

"*What?!*"

"You heard me."

"He was gonna *murder* us!"

"We're letting him go."

Whitmore was staring at him, and the panic was back, a muddy swirl in pain-filled eyes.

Slater's smile was frightening.

"Can't you figure it out, Mr. Whitmore? After these two spread the news around, I have a feeling there'll be some paper out on you. I think you know the kind of paper I mean. My guess is the bounty will be big enough to interest me."

"No!" yelped Whitmore. He clutched feebly at Slater. "No, wait! . . ."

The bounty hunter spun him away from the stage, hitting him in the breadbasket. Whitmore doubled over, wheezing, stumbling, tripping over his own feet. He groveled in the road, drooling blood, whining like a sick dog.

"Let's go," said Slater.

The gun guard was amazed to find himself actually feeling sorry for Whitmore. He would feel sorry for any man who was soon to have Sam Slater on his trail.

As the shotgunner climbed up onto the box, following the reinsman, Slater put the Bible back under his shirt. He retrieved his Spencer and Bryner's repeater, and boarded the coach. The jehu whipped up the six-horse hitch and the stage began to roll, leaving Whitmore in a cloud of white dust.

CHAPTER 24

FOR THE FIRST TIME IN A LONG WHILE, SLATER relaxed. He sat on the forward bench—the smoothest ride—and propped his feet on the opposite seat. His chest hurt, but none of his ribs were cracked. He knew what a cracked rib felt like. He'd been shot, knifed, beaten, kicked, trampled, and just generally roughed up all his life. The way he felt now was old hat.

He was very conscious of the weight of the Bible against his chest. *A close call*, he thought. *Too close.* For the first time in a long while, he thought about God. His survival seemed to exceed the boundaries of luck. Maybe a divine hand had intervened? His mother, a deeply religious person, had always believed that everything, good or bad, happened according to God's plan. As a boy Slater had accepted this; his mother never lied to him.

So believing, he had witnessed the massacre of his parents, suffered the injustice of the incident concerning his uncle, and lived to see his adopted Apache father murdered. Somewhere along this trail of tragedy he reached the conclusion that God did not have very many good things planned for him. Deciding he would be better off without the Almighty's attention, he had discarded his mother's concept as useless baggage, along with his own faith.

Now he began to wonder why he had hauled Hazen's Bible around these last few days. Not because of the .41 Remington derringer; he did not have much good to say for small-caliber hideouts. He hunted men, not jackrabbits. And had he wanted to keep the derringer he could have better carried it in a pocket.

So why this attachment to the big, leatherbound Bible? Why, when he had carried Black Jack Bohannon's two hundred pounds of dead weight across the desert, when every ounce of weight was crucial, had he burdened himself with ten more pounds of The Word? He shook his head, both amused and puzzled by this mystery.

Several miles from the spot he had intercepted the stage, all hell broke loose.

A single shot started it. He knew the kind of gun by the distinctive report, rather like a small cannon. In fact, he had recently heard that exact sound, when the four outlaws had chased him across the *malpais*. Long barrel, big caliber, what was commonly referred to as a "plains rifle".

All this flashed across his mind in an instant. He heard the dying scream of a horse, a shrill cry of fear and alarm from one of the men up top. Then a terrific jolt, the crack of splintering wood—much louder than the rifle shot. Slater braced himself, cursing, as the coach tilted sharply forward, then flipped sideways.

Three hundred yards away, Clyde Bohannon stood beside his horse, the Hawken rifle braced across his saddle, grinning through a drift of pungent powdersmoke as he looked toward the road and witnessed the destruction one well-placed shot had wrought.

He had dropped the offside leader of the six-horse hitch, a sure and certain way to wreck a stage. The coach had flipped completely over several times and now lay on one side, fifty feet from the road. The two men in the box and the dead man on the top rack had hurtled through the air. The hitch, detached from the coach, was a mess of shattered wood, tangled harness, and dead or dying horses.

"Damn," breathed Pop Ogham, standing nearby with his horse.

"Well," said Clyde expansively, "we made quick work of that, didn't we? Glad I inherited this long gun from Three Fingers Smith."

He was well pleased with the way things had worked out. Stony Brown and his three colleagues

had at least managed to put Slater afoot before getting themselves killed, giving him and Pop a chance
at catching up with the bounty hunter, which they
had finally done. All that was left was the retrieval
of Jack's body.

"You won't ever be put on display for all the
good folks to gawk at, brother," he murmured.
Stepping into the saddle, he barked a curt "Come
on."

"I wanted to kill Slater myself," complained
Ogham. He had John Buck's fancy gun and rig
strapped around his waist.

"Christ, Pop," gusted Clyde, exasperated. "You
weren't no match for Sam Slater. You ever killed a
man? Dead is dead."

"He's one tough hombre. Maybe he's still alive."

"No one could live through that. Now come on."

They rode closer, coming first to the body of the
reinsman, whose neck was broken. A few yards
away lay the gun guard. His head had struck a rock,
his skull bursting like a ripe watermelon. Clyde
gazed at this gory scene with complete impassivity.
Pop looked away, his stomach performing somer-
saults; then he saw the money. Greenbacks covered
the ground. The wreck of the stage had hurled Black
Jack's corpse a long way, and the blanket had torn,
spilling cash all over the desert.

Greed glimmering in his rheumy eyes, the old
rewrite man kicked his horse forward, executed a
stumbling dismount, and proceeded to scoop the

money up as fast as he could, stuffing his pockets full, putting more under his shirt.

"What do you think you're doing?"

Pop whirled. Clyde sat his horse, looking sternly down at him.

"I don't recall you riding with us when we took the bank at Hanksville," said Clyde.

Pop noticed the octagonal barrel of the Hawken was aimed in a casual way in his direction.

"And I don't recall you reloadin' that long rifle," he replied.

He reached for the gun on his hip. Clyde was caught by surprise, not expecting Ogham to react in this way; it was totally out of character. He remembered too late that Pop had changed some, virtually overnight, since Mattie's death. Pointing the Hawken at him had just been for effect. Now—too late—he realized it for what it was. A fatal mistake.

Dropping the Hawken, Clyde clutched at his own sidegun, but didn't even clear leather. Pop shot him out of the saddle. Clyde was dead before he hit the ground.

Pop stared at the body for a long time. He had never killed a man before, and the act stunned him. In all his years of criminal activity he had never put himself into a position where he had to. He felt sick. It had been him or Clyde—it was self-defense—but he still felt sick.

The creak of door hinges grated on Pop's nerves. He turned quickly to see the door of the overturned coach open. Sam Slater! Crawling out of the coach, moving real slow, like a man badly hurt. Ogham raised the Texas gunslinger's fancy shooting iron. The range was too great. He started running, then slowed to a walk as Slater pitched off the coach and lay still in the hot sand.

Tough hombre indeed, thought Pop, with grudging admiration. Then he thought again of Mattie. All the rage and hurt came back in a flood. He walked closer, thumbing the hammer back. As he neared, Slater rolled over and sat up, propping himself against the belly of the coach. His face and shirtfront were bathed in blood. A deep scalp line gash was the cause. Pop was scared, but less so when he saw that Slater's holster was empty.

Slater found this out a second later, as he noticed Pop and reached for the absent Schofield. Must have lost it in the wreck. The Bowie knife, once snugged under his belt, was also missing. He'd been tossed around inside the rolling coach like dice in a cup. A cold smile touched his lips as he looked up at Ogham.

Seeing that bloody smile, Ogham shuddered.

"What are you grinnin' at, you bastard?"

"Just thinking."

"About what?"

"God's plan."

"You killed my girl. I'm gonna send you to hell."

Slater didn't bother denying the charge. This man was a thin slice away from pulling the trigger, and Slater couldn't see trying to talk him out of it. He hadn't harmed Mattie Ogham. He wasn't real sure what had happened to her, but saying as much to Pop would sound like begging for his life. To a large degree, Slater lived by Apache rules. One of these was that a man did not show mercy to his enemies, nor did he expect any.

Groping over his head, he grasped one of the thoroughbraces and pulled himself to his feet.

"What are you doing?" yelled Ogham.

"I'll die standing," said Slater flatly.

He reached under his shirt, thinking Pop would surely pull the trigger. He felt every beat of his heart, expecting it to be his last. Why didn't Ogham shoot? Black Jack, Clyde, Stony Brown, almost anybody else would have finished him off quickly. What was Ogham's problem? Maybe killing didn't come easy to this man.

Slowly, almost casually, he pulled out the Bible.

Pop had been in the hideaway cabin when Hazen had taken the derringer out of this Good Book and dispatched one of the Lukan brothers. Had Ogham seen Hazen?

"Drop it!" snapped Ogham.

Apparently he had.

Slater dropped the Bible.

"I'm gonna kill you, Slater."

"Yeah, you keep saying that."

"I am. I swear I'll . . ."

Wincing, Slater reached under his shirt again. Pop saw the powderburn, the bullethole. Slater was gunshot, right in the chest! How could he be above snakes, shot like that?

Then he saw another bullethole appear in Slater's shirt. He heard the sharp crack of a gun going off. Mystified, he looked at the pistol in his hand. He hadn't fired. Who? . . . He tried to say something, but suddenly he couldn't catch his breath. It felt like a steel spike had been hammered through his chest. The pistol slipped out of his grasp. When he saw Slater draw the derringer, still smoking, from under his shirt, he knew the shocking, terrifying truth. He knew it a second, maybe two, before he died.

Slater picked up the Bible, opened it, and deposited the empty Remington within. Kneeling beside Ogham, he laid the Good Book on Pop's chest.

"Don't try to talk a man to death," he said. "Here endeth your lesson."

He stood and glanced up the road, drawn by the sound of a wagon in the distance. A spring wagon, with a canvas cover on a frame over the bed. He had seen it before.

He looked down at himself, at the blood, the grime, the two bulletholes. The one just made was smoldering, he slapped it out. In all that tossing around inside the overturned coach, the over-and-under had fallen out of the Bible. Lucky.

The gun that had once belonged to John Buck, and then briefly to Pop Ogham, went into his empty holster. He caught up both Ogham's horse and Clyde's without difficulty. This, he mused, was a pleasant change!

Hitching the horses to one of the stagecoach wheels, he went over to check what was left of the six-horse hitch. Two of the animals were unhurt. He would have to find that Bowie knife and cut them out of the tangled harness. One of the wheelers was thrashing feebly, a leg broken, big open wounds at hip and stifle gushing blood. Slater put it out of its misery with one shot. *This job*, he thought, *has been hell on the horses.*

The wagon was much closer. He went to meet it. Rachel had the reins. She seemed to be a better hand with a team than Joshua Hazen had been. Instead of two mules she had a pair of horses in harness. She checked them with the sure panache of an experienced teamster, and smiled that quirky smile.

"You look like you'd have to get better to die," said Miss Bounty.

"Where did you get the horses?"

"A man. Had a little place not far from where you left me. It wasn't much farther from there to the spot Hazen and I stashed the wagon."

"What did you do to this man to get the horses?"

"I didn't kill him, if that's what you mean."

"That's not what I meant."

"Why, Sam, you're not jealous, are you?"

Slater didn't dignify that comment with an answer. He checked the back of the wagon, and was some surprised to see the bodies of Stony Brown, Three Fingers Smith, Apache Joe, and John Buck.

"Finders keepers," she said. "Maybe you shot them, but then you left them, fair game."

He gave her a long look. "Rachel . . . you're something else."

"I know."

"You might as well add Clyde Bohannon to your collection."

"You're so nice, Sam. How can I ever repay you?"

She fairly bristled with hardware, gleaned no doubt from the outlaws now resting in the wagon bed. *But she had never*, mused Slater, *been without her greatest weapon.*

"I'm taking Black Jack Bohannon in," he said. "Don't make trouble for me, Rachel."

"I won't."

He looked skeptical, and she waxed indignant.

"What's wrong, Sam? Don't you trust me?"

"No."

"I won't take that personally," she said, stirring up the team. The wagon rolled on by him, turning off the road, heading for the fresh crop of bodies yonder.

Slater shook his head.

"You ought to," he murmured, and started after her.

Saddle-up to these

THE REGULATOR by Dale Colter
Sam Slater, blood brother of the Apache and a cunning bounty-hunter, is out to collect the big price on the heads of the murderous Pauley gang. He'll give them a single choice: surrender and live, or go for your sixgun.

THE REGULATOR—Diablo At Daybreak
by Dale Colter
The Governor wants the blood of the Apache murderers who ravaged his daughter. He gives Sam Slater a choice: work for him, or face a noose. Now Slater must hunt down the deadly renegade Chacon…Slater's Apache brother.

THE JUDGE by Hank Edwards
Federal Judge Clay Torn is more than a judge—sometimes he has to be the jury *and* the executioner. Torn pits himself against the most violent and ruthless man in Kansas, a battle whose final verdict will judge one man right…and one man dead.

THE JUDGE—War Clouds
by Hank Edwards
Judge Clay Torn rides into Dakota where the Cheyenne are painting for war and the army is shining steel and loading lead. If war breaks out, someone is going to make a pile of money on a river of blood.